SCARY
STORIES
FOR WHEN YOU'RE HOME ALONE

ALLEN B. URY

ILLUSTRATIONS BY ERIC REESE

Lowell House House
Juvenile
Los Angeles

CONTEMPORARY BOOKS
Chicago

For "The Ogre"
–A.B.U.

Cover illustration by Bernard Custodio

Library of Congress Catalog Card Number: 96-33902
ISBN: 1-56565-382-3

Publisher: Jack Artenstein
General Manager, Juvenile Division: Elizabeth D. Amos
Director of Publishing Services: Rena Copperman
Editor-in-Chief, Juvenile Fiction: Barbara Schoichet
Managing Editor, Juvenile Division: Lindsey Hay
Art Director: Lisa-Theresa Lenthall

Lowell House books can be purchased at special discounts when
ordered in bulk for premiums and special sales. Contact Department
JH at the following address:

Lowell House Juvenile
2029 Century Park East
Suite 3290
Los Angeles, CA 90067

Manufactured in the United States of America
10 9 8 7 6 5 4 3 2

Contents

SURVIVAL OF THE FITTEST

Dale Chaffin lay tangled in his bed covers. "Up and at 'em!" his Uncle Emory shouted. "Dawn has cracked and it's time for you to get cracking!"

Dale moaned, grabbed his pillow, and slammed it over his head, hoping his uncle would get the message and leave him in peace. Five-thirty in the morning was an ungodly hour for any human being to wake up, let alone a thirteen-year-old who'd been up till 11:00 the night before watching a suspense thriller movie on satellite TV.

But Uncle Emory refused to retreat. Instead, he stepped forward and ripped the covers off Dale's bed.

"I said, get up, Dale! Time's a' wasting!" the big man bellowed. "Today's the day you learn what life and living are all about!"

Dale moaned again, then painfully struggled to lift himself into a sitting position. Uncle Emory tousled the boy's shaggy brown hair, then slapped him heartily on the back.

"There ya go, son," he said approvingly. "Now get yourself showered and dressed. Breakfast is already on the stove. I'm making eggs, bacon, biscuits, and hashbrowns. A *man's* breakfast!"

Tugging at the waist of his camouflage-colored pants, Uncle Emory turned and marched from the room like a soldier ready to do battle. And that comparison wasn't far from the truth, Dale realized. For today, he and his uncle were scheduled to go to war. But their fight would not be with human soldiers or others who were threatening their freedom or way of life. There were no causes here to be championed, no rights to be defended, or territory to be conquered. This war wasn't even about honor.

No, today Dale and his uncle would take up arms against some of nature's most beautiful and harmless creations. They would attempt to erase from the face of the planet creatures whose poise and grace had been celebrated by artists and poets throughout the ages, and who truly embodied the virtues of strength, honesty, and innocence. In other words, Dale and his Uncle Emory were going deer hunting.

That, unfortunately, was not what Dale wanted to do. All he really wanted to do was go back to sleep.

Nevertheless, a half-hour later, Dale was showered, dressed, and sitting at the kitchen table. Before him lay enough food to feed a dozen kids his age, and probably enough fat to clog a sewer pipe. At home, Dale's parents were careful to make sure that their son ate healthy foods. Here, at his uncle's cabin in northern

Minnesota, the idea of "low cholesterol" appeared to be a foreign concept.

"So, Dale, you all set to bag yourself a buck?" Uncle Emory chortled, cheerfully ladling a biscuit with a large portion of gravy. "A set of antlers can look mighty handsome on a young man's wall."

"Actually, I don't feel so good this morning," Dale said weakly. "Maybe you'd better go out alone."

"Nonsense!" Uncle Emory cried. "When your folks dropped you off here for the week, I told 'em I'd make a man out of you, and that's just what I'm going to do. You're going to hunt yourself a deer, and you're going to *like* it!"

"But I don't *want* to be a hunter!" Dale protested. "The whole idea of shooting defenseless animals is so . . ." He searched for the right word. ". . . so *stupid!*"

"*Stupid?*" Uncle Emory blustered. "You ever eat a hamburger, boy? Ever eat a hot dog? Where do you think that meat comes from? Beef trees?"

"That's different," Dale insisted. "When a butcher kills a cow or a pig, he does it to help feed people, not because he thinks it's fun."

"When I kill deer, I eat the venison," Uncle Emory said defensively, referring to deer meat.

"But would you buy venison in the supermarket?" Dale shot back. "Have you ever ordered a Bambi-burger at a restaurant? Of course not. The real reason you hunt deer is because it gives you pleasure. You like to kill. And that's the part I think is sick."

Uncle Emory's eyes narrowed and he leaned his big, 250-pound body over the table toward his young, nervous nephew.

"Let me explain something to you, Dale," he said sternly. "The U.S. Constitution gives me an inalienable right to own and use a gun, and I believe it is the duty of all human beings to do so."

Dale looked confused. "Huh?"

"Humans became the dominant species on this planet for no other reason than they were willing to claim that position through force of arms," his uncle explained slowly. "When some animal killed one of ours, we killed ten of theirs. When a creature tried to eat us, we made sure to eat it first. That's how humans came to be number one." Uncle Emory folded his arms across his big barrel chest. "The name of the game is survival of the fittest. Today, it's up to every one of us to make sure we stay on top by demonstrating our dominance over the animal kingdom."

"You're saying that if we don't go deer hunting, all the deer are going to figure we're weak and try to kill *us?*" Dale asked incredulously. "Like all these forest animals are going to come charging down out of the woods and go rampaging through our cities? Sorry, Uncle Emory, but I don't think so."

"I'm saying that hunting is how a man shows he's a man!" Uncle Emory declared. "Otherwise, we're no better than rabbits! Now finish up and get ready to hit the road."

And so, as soon as they'd cleared the kitchen table, Dale and his uncle hopped into his uncle's Land Rover and sped off into the surrounding woods. Uncle Emory drove only about ten minutes before pulling off into a clearing and killing his engine. He then removed his hunting rifle from the gun rack mounted in the rear of the cab, checked his pockets to make sure he had enough ammunition, then climbed out of the vehicle.

"Which rifle would you like?" he asked Dale, who hadn't moved from his seat.

"I'm not going to do it," the boy responded stubbornly. "I'm not going to murder a poor, defenseless forest creature."

"Fine," his uncle replied, his voice tinged with anger. "But you're not going to sit there all day, either. You're coming with me. As far as I'm concerned, you can think of this as a nature hike."

The way his uncle said "nature hike" was sarcastic enough to let Dale know that he felt nothing but contempt for his nephew's pacifist ideals. But Dale refused to let his uncle get the better of him. Struggling to stay calm, he climbed out of the Land Rover, and made a show of locking his door before closing it.

"Can't be too careful out in the woods," Dale noted, his voice laden with as much sarcasm as his uncle's. "Leave a car unlocked, and those uppity animals might hot wire the thing and take it for a joyride."

"Let's get moving, smart guy," Uncle Emory grumbled, then started off into the nearby pines.

Once they were well off the road, Uncle Emory slowed his pace and began scanning the woods for signs of movement. Dale stayed close behind him, hoping against hope that whatever animal they encountered would have the good sense to run for its life before his uncle had a chance to squeeze off a shot.

Dale was actually beginning to enjoy being out in the cool, moist woods when Uncle Emory raised a hand, motioning him to stop. Looking in the same direction as his uncle, he saw a young deer grazing on the far side of some nearby trees.

Uncle Emory motioned for Dale to keep still, then ever-so-slowly raised his rifle into firing position. Unable to watch, Dale closed his eyes and covered his ears. But what he heard next was not a gun blast. It was a terrible growl. His eyes snapped opened and he saw that the deer had heard it, too. Pricking up its ears, the frightened animal turned and sped off into the woods at lightning speed.

"What the heck was *that?*" Uncle Emory asked, clearly upset.

"I think it was my stomach," Dale answered with an embarrassed grin. "I don't think all the bacon and hashbrowns are digesting very well."

"Well, keep it down!" Uncle Emory grumbled. "You're scaring off the deer!"

With that, the big man moved on. Dale stayed close behind him, pleased with the knowledge that even if his uncle's cooking might someday kill them both, at least on this day it had spared the life of an innocent forest creature.

The next hour passed without incident. Uncle Emory would walk a hundred yards or so, stand still while he scanned the woods for prey, then press on and repeat the ritual a few minutes later. Dale was beginning to think that the whole expedition would prove to be a bust, which would suit him just fine.

Then, while they were starting to circle back toward the Land Rover, Uncle Emory suddenly stopped short and motioned for Dale to do the same.

"What is it?" Dale asked softly.

"Shhhh," Uncle Emory whispered. "There's something out there."

Dale peered toward the trees ahead, but all he could see were trunks, branches, leaves, and mud.

"I don't see anything," he said quietly.

"Something's out there," his uncle stated coldly. "It's watching us. I can feel it."

For the first time all day, a chill ran through Dale's body. And it wasn't from the dampness. Death was in the air. He could smell it. His uncle had come out here to snuff out a life, and one way or another, he was going to have his way.

With aching slowness, Uncle Emory raised his rifle to his shoulder. Gripping the barrel guard with his left hand, he wrapped his right index finger around the trigger, then carefully put his eye to the rifle's telescopic scope.

"I still don't see anything," Dale croaked, his heart pounding like a bass drum. Not knowing what kind of animal his uncle was about to destroy made the suspense even more painful.

"It's there," his uncle insisted. "I can see it moving through the trees."

Dale watched with rising terror as Uncle Emory, moving with the practiced care of a trained marksman, lined up his shot, then squeezed the trigger.

Bang! The shot exploded through the still forest air like a thunderclap. It was so loud that Dale was nearly knocked off his feet. Uncle Emory apparently was equally startled, for he suddenly lost his balance and—*Bang!*—sent another shot flying off wildly into the trees off to his left.

But then a third blast sounded, and instantly it occurred to Dale that the first shot hadn't come from Uncle Emory's rifle. Instead, someone was actually shooting at *them!*

Ka-boom! Another thunderous blast ripped through the air. At virtually the same moment, a chunk of the tree directly to Dale's right exploded into tiny splinters.

"What the—?" Dale exclaimed, but he was unable to finish his thought before another blast ricocheted off a rock close to Uncle Emory's feet, creating a shower of blinding sparks.

"Seek cover!" his uncle shouted.

On the verge of panic, Dale turned and ran like the wind, finally diving behind the wide trunk of a giant oak tree. Uncle Emory joined him a few seconds later.

"What's going on?" Dale cried in terror.

"I don't know," Uncle Emory confessed through breathless gasps. "Some nut is taking pot shots at us!"

"*Who?*" Dale demanded.

"I don't know! I didn't get a look at him," said Uncle Emory as he dug through his pockets for fresh ammo.

Bam! Another shot came screaming through the woods. It glanced off the trunk just a few inches from Uncle Emory's head, taking out a chunk of wood the size of a watermelon.

"That's no rifle he's using," the big man noted. "It's more like a cannon!"

"What are we going to do?" Dale asked, tears now welling up in his eyes.

"We gotta get the heck out of here!" Uncle Emory blubbered. Then he turned, fired off one wild shot, grabbed Dale by the hand, and sped off into the forest.

Leaves and branches whizzed by Dale's face as he and his uncle vaulted through the woods like Olympic sprinters. Behind them, powerful gunshots continued to blast through the air, their impacts often coming dangerously close to bringing down the pair.

Then suddenly, about a half-mile from the Land Rover, Uncle Emory lost his footing. Stumbling weakly, the big man wheezed and groaned as his lungs struggled for air.

"Uncle Emory, what's wrong?" Dale asked fearfully.

"I can't go on," the big man gasped hoarsely. He grabbed the car keys from his pocket and handed them to Dale. "Keep running. Save yourself!"

"No, Uncle Emory!" Dale protested. "I can't leave you here. You *have* to run!"

"I—I can't do it," Uncle Emory said, clearly having trouble getting the words out. "I shouldn't have had that third helping of—"

Just then, Dale heard the sound of something pounding through the woods toward them. The gunman, whoever he was, was approaching fast. Another shot blasted through the air, and Dale instinctively ducked as the bush beside him was blown to twigs.

"I said leave me, Dale!" Uncle Emory screamed. "Save yourself!"

This time, Dale did as he was told. Pumping his arms like twin pistons, he ran across the muddy earth, leapt over gnarled roots, and zig-zagged his way around towering pines.

Finally, he burst out of the forest into the clear-cut path around the road where they had parked. There, just a hundred yards away, was the Land Rover. Hope rising in his heart, Dale was sprinting at full speed for the safety of the car when—*BAM!* Instantly, the ground at his feet exploded in a shower of dirt and debris and Dale was sailing through the air. About twenty feet later, he slammed shoulder first into the ground.

Too stunned to feel any pain, Dale gasped for air and tried to focus his eyes. What he saw nearly caused his heart to stop.

Two beings were walking toward him. Both appeared to be at least seven feet tall, had thin, muscular bodies covered with reptilian scales, and sported oversized heads topped with eyes that hung from stalks like a snail. Both of the nightmarish monsters were dressed in leather-like clothes decorated with dozens of tiny metallic plates, and each carried a long-stemmed object Dale imagined was some sort of alien weapon.

As they approached, each of the creatures raised its firearm and trained it on Dale's helpless body.

I'm going to die, Dale thought, steeling himself. And then one of the beings—the smaller of the pair— addressed the other, its voice echoing directly into Dale's mind.

"I don't want to kill this one, Father," the small creature said in a tone suggesting its confusion. "It looks so young and helpless."

"You're right," the tall one replied, its mouth never moving. "This one is a child. We'll let it go. Better to wait till it grows up . . . and kill it then."

The creatures turned as two more of their kind stepped from the woods carrying Uncle Emory's body trussed up on a pole like some wild game killed on an African safari.

"I still don't understand the point of killing these humans," Dale heard the young one say to its father.

"It's the natural order of things," the older one replied. "It's how a Grezzemblik proves he's a Grezzemblik! Survival of the fittest!"

A moment later, a large, glowing, orange disc appeared above the four creatures. The aliens gathered themselves in a group below it, carrying Uncle Emory's body between them, and the next second, they dissolved in a sparkle of dancing lights.

Back on the ground, Dale just lay there, slack-jawed, unable to believe the scene he'd just witnessed. And then, vowing never to even come near a hunting rifle again, he closed his eyes and was instantly enveloped by the thick, warm blanket of dreamless peaceful sleep.

THE LATE SHIFT

Earthquakes are something you come to expect when living in California. But they're not something you ever really get used to. Maybe that's because, unlike tornadoes, floods, blizzards, hurricanes, or any of the other natural disasters that regularly plague other parts of the United States, earthquakes strike completely without warning. One minute you'll be sitting at your kitchen table having breakfast, the next minute you're bouncing around like you're in the back of a pick-up truck racing down a bumpy highway.

That's what it felt like to Stacey and Suzanne Collins at exactly 3:07 A.M. when the Stockton earthquake hit. One minute the twins were deeply asleep, the next, they were clinging desperately to their mattresses as their beds bucked like wild animals.

"Earthquake!" Stacey shouted to her sister just five feet away as the walls rumbled, the closet doors banged, and books, stuffed animals, and other objects fell off their shelves.

"No kidding!" Suzanne shouted back. "Let's get under the doorframe."

The two girls leaped from their beds and stumbled through the dark to their bedroom doorway. There they hung onto the frame for dear life, like drowning swimmers clutching life preservers.

"I don't feel any safer here, do you?" Stacey cried.

Suzanne shook her head. "Not really, but Dad said it's safer to stand here than in the middle of the room!"

"Let's go to Mom and Dad's room!" Stacey wailed.

"No!" Suzanne insisted, as a desk lamp crashed to the floor. "Let's wait till it's over!"

After what seemed like an eternity, the pitching and rumbling finally subsided. Both sisters let out a collective sigh of relief, and headed down the hall to their parents' bedroom.

"That felt like at least a 5.5," said Suzanne, referring to the 1-to-10-point Richter scale used to measure an earthquake's strength.

"No way," Stacey countered. "It was closer to a six."

"That's odd," Suzanne said, now staring at their parents' closed door. "Why haven't they come out to check on us? They certainly couldn't have slept through all this!" She pushed the door open and turned back to look at her sister, worry in her eyes. "Stacey, Mom and Dad aren't in here."

The two girls stared at their parents' unmade bed.

"Mom? Dad?" Stacey called, thinking that maybe they were in the bathroom. But there was no response. She tried the light switch. The power was out.

Feeling their way through the darkness, the girls checked every inch of the bedroom, the master bathroom, and the large walk-in closet.

"Where could they be?" Suzanne asked.

For the next half hour, the twins raced through the house in a panic. But sometime during the night, Stacey and Suzanne's parents had simply disappeared.

•　•　•

At exactly 3:07 A.M., Robert and Harriet Collins were awakened from their sleep by the violent rattling of their mirrored closet doors. A second later, they felt what they would later describe to friends as "a giant, invisible hand picking up the house and slamming it into the ground over and over again."

As soon as the tremor ceased, Harriet was out of bed and throwing on her robe. "I'm going to check on Suzanne and Stacey," she announced. She flipped the light switch but the lights failed to respond.

"I'll go with you," Robert said, putting on his house slippers in case there was any broken glass on the floor.

They hurried down the hall to the girls' bedroom. The door was open, as usual. In the darkness, they could just make out the outline of the two twin beds.

"Girls?" Harriet called softly as she stepped into the room, flipped another unresponsive light switch, and tripped over a stuffed bear. "Are you okay?"

There was no reply.

"Could they be asleep?" Robert wondered out loud. "That was quite a shaker."

Harriet carefully approached the two beds.

"Robert, they're not here!" she cried.

"I'll get a flashlight," he said, trying to sound calm. But just as he turned to leave, the lights suddenly flickered back on. Robert looked at his wife standing in the middle of the disheveled room. "Did you look under the beds? How about in the closet?"

Harriet nodded grimly. "They're not here," she said.

"Don't panic," Robert said, seeing the fear in her face. "They're somewhere. Maybe they're downstairs."

After a fifteen-minute search of the entire house, there was still no sign of either girl. Both the front and back doors were still deadbolted, and all the windows were closed, indicating that Stacey and Suzanne had not left the house in some kind of panic.

As far as either Robert or Harriet could tell, their daughters had vanished into thin air.

●　●　●

"Stacey, I'm scared," Suzanne groaned. It was now over a half hour since the earthquake, and the twins had failed to find their parents anywhere.

Now seated at the kitchen table, the girls just stared at each other. Then Stacey, being the "Big Sister,"—all of ten minutes older—decided it was her job to be the logical, "mature" one of the pair.

"Let's not panic, okay?" she said calmly. "Both cars are still in the garage. That means they didn't go far."

"Maybe they went next door."

Stacey went to the telephone to call their neighbors, confident that she'd solved the mystery of their missing parents. But when she put the receiver to her ear, a piercing screech greeted her. Startled, she hung up the phone, and tried a second time. But again the phone screamed so loudly it was nearly painful.

"What's wrong with the phone?" Suzanne asked, seeing her sister pull the receiver away from her ear.

But all Stacey could do was look at her sister, her eyes wild with mounting terror.

• • •

"Thanks, Larry, sorry to disturb you. Goodnight," Robert Collins said to Mr. Landers. He hung up the phone and turned back to his wife. "The girls aren't next door," he said grimly.

Harriet took her husband's hand. "What could have happened to our girls?"

"I'm going to check outside." Robert headed for the front closet to get his windbreaker. "Maybe they ran out during the quake."

"Then why are the doors locked?" Harriet asked.

"*I don't know,*" Robert replied, clearly agitated. "I'm just checking out all the possibilities, okay? You stay here in case they show up."

And with that he stepped outside.

• • •

"Boy, it's warm out," Suzanne said as she and Stacey stepped outside into the front yard. "It's like a rain forest."

"Yeah, and the sky has a weird, greenish glow," Stacey said.

"Maybe the quake started some fires," Suzanne suggested half-heartedly.

"Fires make the sky orange, not *green*," Stacey replied. "And listen. It's so—quiet. If there are fires, where are all the fire engines?"

In their thirteen years, both girls had already lived through enough earthquakes to know that each was inevitably followed by a chorus of sirens and car alarms as security systems were tripped and police and fire departments responded to a flurry of emergency calls.

But on this night there was nothing. Absolutely nothing. And this made the sisters even more afraid that something was seriously wrong.

"Stacey, I'm really scared," Suzanne said trembling. "This isn't right. I want to go back into the house."

Stacey, unnerved by the alien, otherworldly sky, was about to follow her sister's suggestion when she noticed a young man about eighteen years old running toward them, waving his arms. It was the first sign of human life she'd seen since the earthquake hit, and something told her that he might hold the answer to their mysterious predicament.

"Go back!" the young man shouted as he approached. "Get back in the house before it's too late!"

"What's going on?" Stacey called to him. "Why is the sky—?"

Before she could finish her sentence, the young man staggered up to them, gasping for air. Stacey immediately noticed that he was dressed oddly. His shirt, pants, and shoes seemed to come from another decade, maybe the '60s or even the '50s.

"Who are you?" Stacey asked.

"My name is Jeff O'Donnell," the young man responded. "I live in that house down the street, number one-twenty-seven."

"No, you don't," Suzanne insisted. "That's the Lowells' house. There's nobody named O'Donnell on this block."

Even as Suzanne spoke, a chill ran down Stacey's spine. She remembered hearing stories about a family named O'Donnell who had lived on their block years ago. Their teenaged son had mysteriously disappeared one day. No trace of him had ever been found.

"Where are we?" Stacey demanded nervously. "What happened to the sky? Why is it so quiet?"

"You're right here in Stockton . . . but then again, you're not," Jeff tried to explain. "I still don't know if I understand it all myself, but every so often, a dimensional shift of some kind occurs in this area, usually during big earthquakes. If you're caught in one, you get separated from everyone else."

"Wh-what do you mean?" Suzanne stammered.

"I mean you can see and respond to inanimate objects, but not to people," Jeff said. "It's like you're traveling down a highway in one traffic lane while everyone else is in another."

"Is that what happened to you?" Stacey asked. "You got caught in this . . . *shift?*"

"In 1963," Jeff said sadly. "There are a few of us here—maybe two dozen total—all from different times. One, a Native American woman, has been here since 1623! And now you're stuck here with us, too."

"But I don't want to be here!" Suzanne shouted. "I want to go home! I want to see my parents again!"

"That's why you've got to get back in the house—now!" Jeff said, pushing them back toward their front door. "There's going to be an aftershock soon. It's your only chance of getting back. You have to be in exactly the same place you were during the earthquake when the first shift occurred. If you miss it, you'll be here for all eternity, just like the rest of us."

Stacey turned back and took Jeff's hand.

"Come with us," Stacey said. "When the aftershock comes, we can all go together."

Jeff shook his head.

"I tried that once, back in 1972," he explained grimly. "A guy appeared after a big quake. We tried to go back together during the next aftershock, but all that happened is that we *both* got stuck here. It's a balance thing. Since you and your sister came through the rift, only you and she can go back."

"Isn't there *anything* we can do?" Stacey asked, seeing the sad, lonely look on Jeff's face.

The young man paused, then unclipped the chain connecting his pocket watch to his belt loop.

"Find my parents. Give them this watch," he said, giving the timepiece to Stacy. "Let them know I'm okay."

As Stacey stared at the beautiful watch, now over three decades old, Suzanne tugged at her arm. "Come on,

Stacey. Hurry up!" she shouted. "We've got to be ready!"

"Good luck!" Jeff called after them as they headed back into their house.

Stacey and Suzanne were halfway up the stairs when the steps seemed to slip out from under them. At the same moment, a thunderous roar filled the air as the very earth beneath their home groaned and shuddered, moved by forces that were far beyond their human comprehension.

"It's the aftershock!" Suzanne shouted.

Stacey's mind exploded with panic. The shift was happening again—but they weren't in their bedroom! They had to make it upstairs and into their beds within seconds if they were ever going to see their parents again. As it was, they might already be too late.

"Hurry!" Stacey shouted. "Run!" She grabbed Suzanne's arm and pulled her off the banister that she was desperately clinging to. Together, they bolted up the swaying staircase, turned into their bedroom, and literally threw themselves onto their beds.

The moment she hit the mattress, Stacey felt a sickening wave of nausea pass over her, and for a brief moment she thought she was falling into a bottomless pit. And then, suddenly, her bed stopped moving, as did the rest of the house. Finally allowing herself to breathe, she turned and looked at Suzanne, who was still clinging to her mattress. "You okay?" she asked.

"I think so," Suzanne whispered. "Do you think we made it in time?"

Stacey hopped off the bed, raced to the window, and opened the blinds. Thankfully, the night sky was normal once again.

"We made it," she sighed with relief.

"What about Mom and Dad?" Suzanne asked, a crack of fear in her voice.

"Let's go see," Stacey replied.

But as she did, their Mom and Dad appeared together in their doorway.

"Stacey! Suzanne!" their mother cried with relief. "Thank goodness!"

The four of them rushed to meet each other and embraced in a strong, almost desperate group hug.

"Where have you been?" their father cried.

"You'll never believe it," Stacey said. And then she looked at Jeff O'Donnell's pocket watch, still grasped in her hand. "Or maybe you will."

At that moment, the closets rattled yet again, and they could all feel the house sway as if bobbing on rough seas. Stacey felt her heart race and a dry, hard lump form in her throat. *It's happening again!* her mind screamed.

But the aftershock passed within seconds, and a quick glance out the window confirmed that she was still in the same, comfortable universe.

"Another aftershock," she said with a nervous laugh as she turned back to her parents. "Felt like about a three point—"

Stacey stopped short. She turned to Suzanne, her face filled with terror. Suzanne, too, looked horrified.

Their mother and father had disappeared.

THE VORTEX

My science teacher, Mr. Lombardo, is always introducing us to weird gadgets. Today he's got this bizarre-looking box about the size of a large toaster oven. He says, "This machine is called an electroencephalogram, or EEG for short. It's designed to record brain waves. Does anyone know what brain waves are caused by?"

Many hands go up—all except mine.

Mr. Lombardo scans the class, then looks directly as me. "Kevin, can you tell me what causes brain waves?" he asks.

I've been only half paying attention—as usual—so I respond with the first thing that pops into my mind: "Uh, brain tides?"

This gets a big laugh from the class. I smile, and take a bow, pleased that I scored some points with my friends. Mr. Lombardo, however, is not amused at all.

"This is neither the time nor the place for humor, Kevin," he says sternly. "Step up to the front of the room, please."

"Why?" I respond defensively. I've smarted-off in front of Mr. Lombardo enough times to know he has some kind of punishment in mind, and I'd like to know what to prepare for.

"I'm going to perform a little experiment," Mr. Lombardo says, smiling coldly. "I want to see if that brain of yours is actually working after all."

This time, it's Mr. Lombardo who gets the laugh. So that's what this is about, eh? It's a contest between him and me. Well, I can accept that. In fact, I welcome it. I just hope he realizes that, when it comes to war, I take no prisoners.

"All right," I say, putting on a cheerful expression. "Let's do it."

Jumping to my feet, I bound up to the front of the classroom and, grinning widely, thrust my fists into the air like a boxer who has just entered the ring. I can sense the other kids cheering me on. I'm the "David" set to do battle with the "Goliath" Mr. Lombardo. If I can hold my own, I'll be the class hero.

As I join Mr. Lombardo at his desk, thunder rumbles in the distance and I notice raindrops on the classroom windows. A storm is coming. A big one.

"All right, Kevin, I'd like you to sit down in my chair if you would please," he says dryly.

"*Your* chair?" I respond with surprise. "Hey, I like this already!"

I saunter over to his desk, plop myself down in his chair, then casually put my feet up on his desk.

"Put both feet on the floor," he orders, as the other kids struggle to suppress their giggles.

"No problem," I say, then sit up straight, hands folded in front of me, like a regular Goody-Two-Shoes. This gets an even bigger laugh than when I put my feet on his desk. So far, I am definitely ahead in points.

"Now, I just want you to relax. Don't move," Mr. Lombardo instructs. "I'm going to fit a sensor cap onto your head."

He picks up what looks like a rubber swimming cap with two dozen wires running from it. Positioning himself behind me, he begins to force the tight-fitting contraption over my head.

"Ouch!" I cry as the cap pulls on my long, shoulder-length hair.

"It's supposed to be tight," Mr. Lombardo explains. "Please, hold still."

After tugging and pulling for what seems like five minutes, Mr. Lombardo finally gets the cap over my head. I can feel it pressing on all parts of my skull, and it's starting to give me a headache. Outside, the wind and rain have increased. Lightning flashes, and thunder booms nearby. Between the storm and this EEG thing, I feel like something out of an old Frankenstein movie.

"Now, Kevin, if you had read your textbook, you'd know that brain waves are caused by electrochemical impulses between the nerve cells in your brain," Mr. Lombardo says, addressing this to both me and the class. "The more active various parts of your brain are, the stronger the wave activity. What this EEG is going to do is measure that activity."

"Cool," I say, still not quite sure what the guy is talking about. "Measure away."

Mr. Lombardo flips a switch on the EEG box and it hums into life. Lights dance across its control panel, and a piece of paper with all kinds of wavy lines on it begins to slowly emerge from a slot on its side.

"Sit back and relax, Kevin," Mr. Lombardo says in a low, soothing voice. As instructed, I settle back in his leather chair, fold my hands over my stomach, take a deep breath, and shut my eyes. "Now, try to clear your mind of all thoughts," he says, adding, "For you, that shouldn't be too difficult."

There's another ripple of laughter from the class, and I realize I've got some serious work to do if I'm going to win this battle of wits.

Shutting my eyes, I slap a big, goony smile on my face, like a guy who's just stretched himself out on a hammock to enjoy a beautiful summer's day lazing in the sun. I want Mr. Lombardo to know that I'm enjoying myself immensely.

"First, I want you to imagine something peaceful. Something beautiful," Mr. Lombardo says. "Picture yourself lying out on a warm, sandy beach."

"No problem," I chortle. And it isn't one. As a matter of fact, this was pretty close to what I was thinking about when he called on me in the first place.

Cracking open my left eye, I catch a glimpse of my teacher studying the pattern of wavy lines on the paper that is slowly rolling out of the EEG machine. Then another bolt of lightning flashes and a thunder boom breaks my concentration, and I try to settle myself back into the chair.

"All right," Mr. Lombardo continues. "Now I want you to think about something terrifying . . . something like monsters."

Closing my eyes, I imagine the room's windows exploding outward and a huge, tentacled beast reaching in and grabbing Mr. Lombardo around the throat. He screams and struggles, only to be crushed like an empty soft drink can.

"Now, I want you all to take a look at how these brain wave patterns have changed—" Mr. Lombardo says, when all of a sudden there's a flash so blinding I can see it even through my closed eyelids. A split second later, the room is hit with a thunder crash so loud I think a bomb has just gone off.

At the same time, I feel a surge of energy flood into my head. Instantly, my eyes pop open. Next to me, the EEG machine explodes in a blinding shower of sparks. I feel like I'm hit with a giant, invisible hand, and I crash backward onto the floor.

Then everything goes dark. *Am I dead?* I wonder. *Is this what death feels like?*

I'm looking around, trying to get my bearings, when Mr. Lombardo's face suddenly looms over me.

"Kevin, are you all right?" he asks, his voice oddly distorted. If I *am* dead, then Mr. Lombardo must have died, too. "Try to sit up," he says, lifting me into a sitting position.

I see now that I'm still in our science classroom and from the looks of things, still very much alive. All the lights are out, but there's enough cold, gray light coming in from the windows to see by. Flashes of lightning briefly illuminate the faces of the students

silently staring at me, giving them an eerie, ghostlike appearance that really creeps me out.

"Wh-what happened?" I stammer, still trying to keep my head from spinning.

"The school was just struck by lightning," Mr. Lombardo explains. "Apparently, the power surge blew out the EEG. I think some of the electricity might have gone into your skullcap as well. Did you feel a shock?"

"I sure felt *something*," I say with a nervous laugh, ripping that tight-fitting sensor cap from my head. "It was pretty wild."

"I'd like you to go down and see the nurse, just to make sure you're okay," Mr. Lombardo says, hurriedly writing me a hall pass. "When it comes to electricity, I don't like taking chances."

"Why, what do you think it could have done to me?" I ask, intentionally twitching my shoulders and scrunching up one side of my face.

"That's not funny," he responds. "Now give this note to the nurse and—"

Suddenly, the window behind him explodes. Several kids scream as shards of broken glass go flying all over the room. At first, I think the building's been hit by lightning again, or maybe a tornado has just touched down. But then, to my horror, I see a huge, dark form rise into view outside and a huge tentacle covered with little suction cups comes snaking its way through the broken pane.

Mr. Lombardo sees it too and tries to run, but the monstrous arm grabs him and begins hauling him toward the window. Screaming hysterically, the other kids abandon their desks and bolt for the door, pushing and shoving in a mad rush to escape this nightmarish creature. As for me, I just stand there in silent horror, realizing that this monster is the very same one I was imagining just before the lightning struck. I'm still standing there as I watch the creature crush Mr. Lombardo like an empty soft drink can. Then I nearly throw up when it tosses his lifeless body into its drooling mouth.

This can't be happening! my mind screams. *I must still be unconscious and imagining this!*

A moment later, the creature's tentacle returns and makes a grab straight for me. Imaginary or not, I'm not about to hang around and watch myself wind up like Mr. Lombardo. Spinning on my heels, I dive for the door and barely make it through right behind the last of my classmates.

Out in the main corridor, I'm surprised to see kids pouring out of the other classrooms, too, running and screaming in an uncontrolled panic. I grab one of these other kids, a red-haired seventh grader, and scream, "What's happening? What's everyone running from?"

"The monster!" the kid screams. "It came through the window! It ate two kids! Run for your life!"

His eyes filled with mortal terror, the poor kid yanks himself free and joins the panic-stricken crowd streaming for the exits.

Now I'm *really* confused. The monster that ate Mr. Lombardo—the one I had first imagined while wearing the EEG cap—had attacked from the south side of the school. But the seventh-grader had run from a room facing *north*. He couldn't be talking about the same monster I'd seen. Could there be *another*?

My question is immediately answered when I glance toward the room the kid had escaped from and see a creature even more horrifying than the one that had invaded our classroom. This one stands on two huge, spindly legs like a flamingo's, has a body like a beach ball, and has a snakelike head with a long, jagged beak that it's using to grab, smash, and swallow all the desks in the room.

"Yikes!" I scream, then sprint madly toward the exit. As I run past another classroom, a *third* monster leaps out and makes a grab for me. This one looks like an eight-foot-tall jackrabbit, but it has huge, orange eyes like a housefly's, and its oversized jaws are filled with multiple rows of large, jagged teeth.

Somehow, I elude the terrible creature's grasp, make it to the stairwell and, joining the flood of hysterical kids and teachers who are still thundering down the halls, run out into the pouring rain.

Pushed and shoved through the parking lot by the stream of fleeing students, I'm a full half-block away from the junior high before I'm able to turn and look back. When I do, I can hardly believe my eyes. Directly above the school, storm clouds are swirling in a tight circle. There's a weird, green glow coming from the center of this airborne whirlpool, and flashes of lightning crackle within it.

I'm no scientist, but I know this is no natural event. Something extraordinary is going on, and my guess is it's related to both that terrible lightning strike and the EEG cap. Maybe the power surge allowed my brain to tear an opening between our world and some horrible parallel universe. Maybe it caused the deepest, darkest parts of my own subconscious mind to be brought to life. Or maybe I'm still knocked out, and this is nothing but my own private nightmare from which I will soon awake.

Whatever the real explanation is, it will have to wait. The whirlpool—this vortex—is growing larger even as I watch it. And as it grows, more and more hideous monsters are appearing around the school. Some look like mutant lizards or disfigured dinosaurs. Others are massive insects the size of school buses. And one, which comes barreling out of the school's main entrance, looks like nothing but a huge ball of fur with fangs.

Like an advancing army, the monsters fan out from the school, destroying everything in their path. They uproot trees like a gardener yanking weeds. They crush whole cars flat beneath their massive feet. And many of the hideous creatures are scooping up dozens of kids in their steam shovel-like mouths and swallowing them down whole.

Too frightened to even think straight, I run at top speed out of the parking lot and down Central Street. All around me, cars are careening off the road and crashing into each other as their startled drivers find the road ahead blocked by a monster stampede. One minivan nearly runs me down, but I'm able to jump out of the way just before its driver, shocked by a huge pink flying jellyfish landing with a splat on his windshield, loses control and crashes headlong into a hundred-year-old oak tree.

My lungs aching, I somehow make it back to my house. The screams of my fellow schoolmates are still ringing in my ears as I fumble for my keys and let myself in. Just before I slam and lock the door, I look up and see the glowing vortex growing ever larger. At this rate, it will soon engulf the entire sky.

This is all my fault! My mind screams as I fall against the front door, gasping for breath. *My own mind made all of this horrible stuff happen. If the world ends, it will be because of me!*

Looking out my front window, I see a half-dozen people running wildly down the street being chased by a ratlike monster hopping on a pair of huge, kangaroo legs. Behind it, a blue, fuzzy caterpillar the size of a railroad car is eating up the trees that line our block.

Suddenly, it occurs to me that my mom and dad are still away at work. In another hour they'll try to come home, only to find their neighborhood overrun by nightmare monsters. That is, if they even get this far. If I'm right—if the vortex grows until it covers the entire planet—my parents could be dead before they even leave their offices.

That means, if I'm to survive—and save the world—it's up to me to *uncreate* everything that my mind has created.

I'm working feverishly to think of exactly what to do when I hear something clawing at the door. Instantly, I jump away in terror. The clawing continues, but the door holds—for now.

I've got to see what it is. I want to know what's trying to get into my house. Screwing up my courage, I venture cautiously into the living room and pull back the drapes to get a look at the front stoop. Only I can't see the stoop. I can't even see the front yard. All I can see are two huge eyes—eyes as big as billboards—and they're looking right back at *me*!

All at once, my course of action suddenly becomes painfully clear. I've always wanted to be a hero, and here's my chance.

Sucking in my final lungful of air, I march to the front door, grab the handle, and pull it open. Instantly, the monster's hot, foul breath surrounds me and I'm seized in the grip of a huge, powerful tongue. The next second, everything goes dark . . . and the nightmare finally comes to an end.

HERESY

Judge Nathaniel Gravestone slammed his gavel. "Bring in the accused!" he ordered.

Everyone in the small, makeshift courtroom turned to the doors located along the back wall. After a few moments, two officers dressed in dark, seventeenth century uniforms appeared and marched their prisoner up the center aisle.

Unlike the thieves, pickpockets, and brawlers who had been brought before Judge Gravestone earlier in the day, this prisoner didn't look at all like someone who would run afoul of the law. She was a girl—by the looks of her no more than thirteen years old—dressed in the pale, simple clothing typical of the Puritans who had settled in this part of the New World since the Mayflower's arrival at Plymouth approximately twenty years before. Clearly frightened, the girl kept her large, brown eyes cast downward as she was led up to the front of the courtroom and directed to stand on a small wooden platform.

In the gallery, those townspeople who had come to watch the trial shifted nervously in their chairs and exchanged excited whispers. Many onlookers wore expressions of fear or hatred, as if this seemingly harmless maiden carried some wretched disease that could destroy them all.

"Charity Stamford," the judge intoned, looking down at his notes but directing his words toward the girl standing not ten feet away. "You have been accused by the good people of this village of practicing supernatural arts and engaging in other activities in violation of the laws of nature. Tell me, young lady, how do you plead?"

"Leave my child alone!" a woman cried from the courtroom gallery. This was Charity's mother, known in town as The Widow Stamford since her husband had reportedly died during the crossing from England the previous year. A thin, plain-featured woman in her early thirties, her dry, furrowed skin was marked by a lifetime of hard work and stern discipline. "My little girl is innocent! The charges are untrue!"

"Silence!" Judge Gravestone ordered, hammering his gavel on the bench before him. "This court will determine what is true and what is not!" Collecting himself, he turned back to the accused. "Now, Miss Stamford, as to the charge of engaging in the supernatural, how do you plead?"

"Not guilty," Charity replied, her dark brown eyes still downcast, her voice barely a whisper.

"You will have to speak much louder, girl," the stern magistrate instructed.

"Not guilty," Charity stated for all to hear.

"Very well, child," Judge Gravestone grumbled, seemingly unconvinced. He turned to a tall, long-haired young man wearing the uniform of a court prosecutor. "Mr. Bainbridge, you may call your first witness."

Rising, Mr. Bainbridge straightened his black coat, then shouted as if wishing to be heard all the way back to England, "The People call Miss Hope Duckworth to the stand!"

For the past six years, Miss Duckworth had served as the one and only teacher at the small, one-room school in which all the children of this Pilgrim village were educated. A prim, prune-faced woman whose thin, gray hair was pulled tightly back behind her head, she marched eagerly to the witness box where she was sworn to tell the truth and nothing but.

"Now, Miss Duckworth, you are one of those good citizens who have accused Charity Stamford of being a sorceress," Mr. Bainbridge began, posing proudly before the judge. "Please tell this court what the defendant did to lead you to this conclusion."

"I was teaching English grammar and composition to my middle-schoolers," Miss Duckworth replied, her posture as straight as the ruler she regularly wielded against her most unruly students. "And as a writing exercise, I asked the students to construct an essay in which they were to describe what life might be like here in the Massachusetts Bay Colony three hundred years hence."

"Naturally, you expected an essay imagining a society devoted to prayer, study, and the doing of charitable works," the prosecutor suggested.

"Of course," the teacher said. "With the proper spelling and punctuation, of course."

"Of course," Mr. Bainbridge said, now turning his gaze toward Charity Stamford, who was shivering nervously as she clutched the wooden railing before her. "And was this what the defendant wrote?"

"No, sir, it was not," Miss Duckworth reported. "The things she wrote about—well, I dare hardly speak of them in mixed company!"

"This is a court of law, Miss Duckworth," Judge Gravestone reminded the teacher. "You are compelled to relate the facts as you know them."

Miss Duckworth twisted her wrinkled lips as if tasting something foul, then spoke rapidly. "She wrote of a time when this village would be home to not only Englishmen, but also to Indians, Africans, Spanish, and even Chinese, all living as equal individuals in the same community."

The townsfolk in the gallery recoiled in terror.

"Go on," Mr. Bainbridge prompted.

"She wrote of men and women traveling the streets in horseless carriages, of winged ships flying through the air like birds, and of people speaking directly to one another over vast distances by holding objects to their ears and mouths," Miss Duckworth went on, eyeing

Charity sternly. "Either the girl is just headstrong or she's simply speaking—"

"Heresy!" one of the townspeople shouted.

"Sorceress!" another cried.

"Off with her head!" a third demanded.

"Did you ask Charity where she got such outrageous notions?" Mr. Bainbridge inquired.

"Of course," Miss Duckworth replied haughtily. "She claimed she had a vision."

Now virtually everyone in the gallery was on their feet, screaming for Charity Stamford's death. In the center of the near-riot, Charity's mother sat sobbing into a lace handkerchief. Twenty feet away, Charity cowered as several spectators hurled chunks of rotted fruit and vegetables her way.

"Order!" Judge Gravestone shouted, slamming his gavel repeatedly. "I will have order in this courtroom this very instant!"

Slowly, the angry mob quieted down and returned to their seats. Standing by the witness box, Mr. Bainbridge smoothed the folds of his dark coat, then directed Miss Duckworth back to her seat.

"Thank you, Miss Duckworth," he said formally. "I have no further questions."

Mr. Bainbridge's next witness was William Franklin Hooke, a classmate of young Charity's. After putting the trembling boy under oath, Bainbridge had the handsome, fourteen-year-old youth recount a dream the girl had related to him just a few weeks earlier. Initially reluctant to testify against his friend, William nonetheless described Charity's dream as best he could remember it.

"She said that in her dream, we no longer lived under the crown of England. She claimed we were a free people unto ourselves," William reported, his head bowed shamefully.

"Traitor!" several men cried from the gallery.

"String her up!" another demanded.

"She said that the people of this land were free to speak as they so desired, worship as they please, and write and read without official censors," young William went on.

"Blasphemy!" shouted a bearded man.

"Hang her!" cried a round-faced woman.

"And did she say that this was, after all, only a dream?" Mr. Bainbridge inquired.

William hesitated a long moment, threw Charity a look as if to ask her forgiveness, then turned to face the humorless prosecutor. "No, sir," he replied nervously. "Charity said she believed this is the way our land will be someday."

A moment later, the courtroom erupted into chaos. It took everything the uniformed officers could do to bring the angry citizens under control. One particularly angry farmer even managed to grab hold of Charity's arm before a guard got the man in a headlock and wrestled him away.

"One more outburst like that and I shall see you all in the stockade!" Judge Gravestone roared as the other officers slowly got the room back under control. He cleared his throat and looked at the prosecutor. "Now, Mr. Bainbridge, do you have any more questions for this witness?"

"No, Your Honor," Bainbridge replied with a bow.

"Then the witness is excused," the judge ordered.

The prosecution's third and final witness was Abigail Stamford, Charity's younger sister. The shy, blond-haired eleven-year-old was clearly reluctant to testify against her big sister, but Judge Gravestone reminded the girl that it was her duty to expose evil wherever she found it, even when it resided under her own roof.

"Earlier this year, you and your sister talked about the future, did you not?" Mr. Bainbridge began gently.

"Yes, sir," young Abigail replied forthrightly, her posture straight, her eyes clear.

"You were talking about what you could be when you grow up, isn't that right?" Mr. Bainbridge probed.

"Yes, sir," Abigail responded.

"And tell me, dear, what did Charity, your older sister, tell you that you could be?" the prosecutor asked, looking disdainfully toward the accused.

"She said I could be anything I wanted," Abigail said painfully.

The spectators responded to this with a collective gasp. Of all the outrageous statements they had heard so far, this was by far the most shocking.

"*She said you could be anything you wanted,*" Mr. Bainbridge repeated, as if unable to believe the statement himself. "Did she mean you could perhaps marry above your station? Or that you could work as a school teacher?"

"No, sir," Abigail replied, a frightened quiver in her voice. "She said that girls should be as equals to boys. That we could grow up to be farmers, physicians, even lawyers and magistrates as we so choose."

At this, Judge Gravestone turned deep red. He looked like he was about to pop every blood vessel in his stout, flabby body. "Enough!" he finally bellowed. "This court has heard enough!" He turned to Charity. "Miss Stamford, before this court issues its verdict and pronounces its sentence, it shall give you one chance and one chance only to renounce all the blasphemous things you have said."

"Sir?" Charity responded, for she did not quite understand the judge's statement.

"I'm giving you a chance to take it all back," Judge Gravestone said imploringly. "All this nonsense about rebellion against the Crown, winged ships, uncensored books, and women magistrates. Deny it all! Tell this court it was nothing but a bad dream! For I can tell you right now, Charity Stanford, that if you don't renounce this heresy this very moment I will have no choice but to sentence you to death!"

Charity scanned the faces in the room. She saw the fear and contempt in the eyes of the townspeople she had known all her life. The agony of her mother. The shame and confusion of her sister Abigail. As a girl who had always devoted her life to truth and honor, she knew what she had to do.

"Very well, Your Honor," she said, sitting tall and looking Judge Gravestone straight in the eye. "I do renounce these claims. They were childish fantasies. Nothing but fairy stories. They have no more weight than the air we breathe."

With that, Judge Gravestone breathed a huge sigh of relief, as did Charity's mother, her sister Abigail, and William Hooke.

"Then all charges are dismissed," the judge declared with a bang of his gavel. "And this court stands adjourned."

As everyone filed out of the room, Charity's mother and sister ran to the defendant's box and threw their arms around the young girl.

"You foolish child!" her mother said harshly. "How could you talk of such things? You must never, ever speak of the future this way again! You could have gotten us all killed!"

"I am truly sorry, Mother," Charity apologized. "I had no idea these people would react so."

"An entire year in the New World, and you've learned nothing!" her mother chastised her. "Sometimes I wonder why I even bothered to pay for this expedition."

"You said it was for our education," young Abigail reminded her. "To make us understand and appreciate early American history by living a part of it."

"And instead, you brought glimpses of the future to people who are wholly unable to appreciate it," Charity's mother said critically. "I fear that if we stay here any longer, we will critically damage the timeline—or worse!"

"I'm truly sorry, Mother," Charity said again, bowing her head.

"Tell it to your father when you get home," her mother snapped, then grabbed both her daughters by the arm and hurried them from the building.

Later that evening, in a cave unknown to the local settlers, Charity, Abigail, and their mother returned to the twenty-first century time machine that had deposited them here in New England in 1655, one year ago. A few minutes later, they and their vehicle vanished in a brilliant flash of light, never to return.

Unknown to any of them, William Hooke had followed them to this site, and gasped in awe as the Stamfords and their unworldly machine disappeared into thin air. Remembering what Charity *had* said about horseless carriages, free speech, and careers for women, he reached the only logical conclusion he could: Charity had been dealing in the supernatural after all . . . with the aim of confusing and confounding the good people of Massachusetts Bay with visions of a future which could never come to pass.

OUIJA SPEAKS

Randy Parkes leaned over his neighbor's shoulder. "What are you working on now, Mr. Lessing?" he asked.

Randy had lived next door to old Mr. Lessing for all of his fourteen years. And for most of that time, Mr. Lessing had spent virtually all his waking hours in the workshop he'd built in his garage. Before he retired, Mr. Lessing had been an engineer for a huge aerospace company that made supersonic jet fighters, top-secret spy satellites, and the powerful three-stage rockets that sent men and machines hurtling into outer space.

But now, comfortably in his mid-seventies, Mr. Lessing preferred to spend his days working with his hands, building all kinds of models from scratch. More interested in actually building the models than collecting them, Mr. Lessing usually let Randy or his kid brother Sean keep the finished products for themselves when he was done. As a result, Randy had the coolest collection of handcrafted airplanes, ships, cars, and spacecraft in the entire eighth grade.

"Well, my boy," Mr. Lessing said, removing his plastic protective goggles from his ruddy-cheeked face and wiping his eyes with a handkerchief, "I've decided to make something useful this time."

"You mean like a salad bowl?" Randy asked.

"No, no, no, nothing so ordinary!" Mr. Lessing said with a laugh. "No, for most of my life, I've had an interest in the supernatural—ESP, spirit channeling, that sort of thing. I suppose it was a reaction to the 'hard science' I was forced to practice every day. All those numbers and formulas—they can drive you crazy after a while! No, I've always believed that the human soul requires more than mere mathematical certainty. It needs a sense of, well, *mystery*."

Flashing Randy a knowing smile, he motioned the boy into his garage. The space was cluttered with all kinds of power tools, woodworking equipment, and models in various stages of completion. In fact, there was so much clutter that Mr. Lessing had long ago taken to parking his car in his driveway, leaving the garage exclusively for his hobbies.

"Here it is," Mr. Lessing said with pride as he whisked a towel off one of his workbenches with a theatrical flourish; "My latest masterpiece!"

There on the bench sat a wooden board the size of a lunch tray. Its highly polished surface was inlaid with two rows of letters, A thru Z, under which was a row of numbers going from 0 to 9. In the upper left-hand corner was a smiling "Man in the Moon" labeled "Yes." In the opposite corner was a frowning moonface labeled

"No." Between them were the words "Can't Say," and at the bottom was the message, "Goodbye."

"A Ouija board!" Randy exclaimed, recognizing it instantly. "A friend of mine got one for his birthday."

"A cheap, mass-produced piece of plywood, no doubt," Mr. Lessing said, scoffing. "*This* board is a work of art. It's got mother-of-pearl inlays, and the planchet is made from lacquered teak with a lead crystal viewport—*not* plastic, like most others."

"What's a 'planchet'?" asked Randy.

Mr. Lessing held up the heart-shaped platform on which players poised their fingers to make the board spell out its messages.

"Oh, the pointer thing," Randy said, immediately noticing that it looked more like a piece of fine sculpture than something stamped out at a toy factory. "Can I touch it?" he asked, extending his hands.

"Of course," said Mr. Lessing, dropping the planchet into Randy's waiting palms. Although the piece was firm and solid, it was surprisingly light.

Just the right weight for spirits, Randy thought.

"In fact," said Mr. Lessing, continuing, "you can have the entire set, board and all."

"I can keep it?" Randy said with surprise.

"You keep everything else I make, don't you?" Mr. Lessing noted with a grin.

"But those are just models," Randy replied. "This is a work of art. You put so much into it . . ."

"My heart and soul," Mr. Lessing admitted. "But I'm a busy man. When would I have time to commune with the spirit world? No, I made this for you and your brother with one condition."

"What?" Randy asked cautiously.

Mr. Lessing leaned into Randy and spoke softly. "If the spirits tell you who's going to win next year's Super Bowl, let me know."

●　●　●

That evening, after they'd eaten dinner and done their homework, Randy and his ten-year-old brother Sean sat on the edges of their twin beds facing each other, Mr. Lessing's Ouija board between them balanced on their knees.

"So how's this supposed to work?" Sean asked.

"We put this planchet thing on the board, then we lightly rest our fingers on it," Randy explained. "Then we ask it a question, and it spells out the answer."

"What makes it move?" Sean wanted to know.

"That's the mystery," Randy replied. "Some say it's spirits of the dead. Others say it's just our subconscious minds. You wanna try it?"

"Sure," Sean said, sitting up straight. He placed his fingers lightly on the heart-shaped planchet and Randy did the same.

They sat that way for several awkward seconds until Randy finally blurted out. "Well, what do you want to ask it?"

"I don't know. What do *you* want to ask it?"

"I don't know. Let me think," Randy said. He considered the problem for a few seconds, then announced, "Ouija board, can you hear us?"

The room remained deathly quiet for several more seconds as the brothers stared at the board, awaiting a reply. Then, to their surprise, the wooden planchet beneath their fingers moved slightly.

"You did that," Sean said accusingly.

"I didn't," Randy insisted. "Keep concentrating."

Again the boys stared at the planchet. After several tense seconds, the marker slid slowly to the upper left-hand corner of the board, indicating "Yes."

"It hears us!" Sean gasped.

"All right, Ouija board," Randy said excitedly. "Who's going to win next year's Super Bowl?"

There was another moment of silence, then the planchet moved again. This time, it settled into the middle of the board and stopped over the letter "P."

"Pittsburgh?" Randy asked expectantly. Again the marker moved, this time pausing over the letter "A."

"What team begins with P-A?" Sean asked his brother. "Panthers?"

"There are no 'Panthers' in professional football," Randy said with irritation. Even as he spoke, the planchet continued to spell out its reply. It paused over the letter "R", then went on to K-I-N-G-L-O-T. Finally, it slid into the space marked "Goodbye" and stopped.

Randy shrugged. "*Parking lot?*"

"Maybe it's broken," Sean said with a yawn. "Anyway, I'm getting tired. Let's try again tomorrow."

"Suits me fine," Randy agreed, sliding Mr. Lessing's board under his bed.

The next morning, the local news was on the kitchen TV when the boys came down for breakfast. Neither Randy nor Sean were particularly interested in current events—unless it had to do with sports—so they barely paid attention to the broadcast. However, the story of a local murder, thought to be the third in a series, caught their attention. According to the report, the victim—a nursing student—had been killed in her college parking lot.

"The *parking lot!*" Sean whispered to Randy as they headed off to their respective schools. "Just like the Ouija board said!"

"It's a coincidence. It could mean anything," Randy said dismissively. "After all, we asked it about the Super Bowl, remember?"

Randy knew that the odds of Mr. Lessing's Ouija board knowing something about the string of local murders were one in a billion. Still, he couldn't shake the uneasy feeling that maybe—just *maybe*—there was a connection. And it sure gave him the creeps.

●　●　●

That evening, after dinner, the brothers again perched themselves on the edges of their beds and set the handcrafted spirit board between them. Almost immediately, Sean blurted out his question.

"Ouija board, do you know who killed the nursing student last night?" he inquired. After a brief moment, the planchet slid quickly over to the "Yes" spot.

Randy gasped, realizing they might have stumbled onto something. "OK, Ouija board, who's the killer?"

Sliding beneath their fingertips, the planchet moved to the spot designated "Can't Say."

"Can't say or *won't* say?" Sean demanded. Now the planchet slid over to the alphabet section where it quickly spelled out R-I-V-E-R.

"Is that the killer's name? River?" Sean asked.

"I don't think so," Randy said nervously. "In fact, I think that's where he's going to kill next."

When the board refused to respond to any further questions, the brothers were forced into the difficult position of having to decide what to do with the critical but otherwise vague clue they had just been handed.

Sean wanted to call the police, but Randy knew that the cops would never believe them. They were two dumb kids who were talking to a Ouija board, for crying out loud! At best, the police would think they were simply crazy. At worst, they might suspect the two were trying to pull some kind of juvenile prank.

In the end, they decided to simply wait to see if the prediction came true. And happily, the next morning they could find no news about any more murders in the newspaper or on TV. By that afternoon, they came to the conclusion that their Ouija board was nothing but a good-looking toy that was simply responding to subtle hand movements they didn't even know they were making. As for the "parking lot" message, well, it probably *was* just a coincidence.

Yes, that was their conclusion . . . until one day later, when the news reported that the body of an elderly man had been pulled from the local river the night before. Once again, the evidence pointed to the serial killer.

"The Ouija board was right!" Sean said beaming. "It knows where the killer is going to strike next!"

"This is too weird," Randy said grimly. "Why *our* Ouija board? And why *us*? What good is this information if we're too young to do anything about it?"

"Who knows," Sean said. "But we have to keep on this. Maybe we can stop the killer before he strikes the next time!"

● ● ●

As they did every Friday night, Randy and Sean's parents went out to dinner and a movie . . . alone. Ever since Randy was old enough to take care of himself and Sean—just last year, actually—this was his parents' "Date Night," and although the brothers weren't exactly thrilled about staying home by themselves with a mad killer on the loose, they knew their parents relished their evenings out, so they didn't protest. Besides, there was no way that Randy was going to have a baby-sitter. No, if they kept the doors and windows locked, he and Sean would be perfectly safe.

Just after seven o'clock, Randy and Sean finished the pizza their parents had left them. At the same time, a storm front moved in, bringing with it howling winds, slashing rain, and bursts of thunder and lightning.

It was a perfect night for a murder. And that's why Sean insisted they get out the Ouija board to find out where the next killing was going to be.

"Let's just leave well enough alone," Randy said.

"Then I'll do it myself!" Sean said, racing upstairs to their bedroom.

Randy sighed and turned on the TV. He didn't want anything more to do with serial killers or Ouija boards. In fact, he had a good notion to give the board back to Mr. Lessing first thing in the morning. The old guy had made it. He should be the one to deal with it.

Randy had just gotten comfortable in his dad's easy chair when a brilliant lightning flash flared directly outside the living room window. A split second later, the house was shaken by an explosive crash of thunder and every light in the house went off.

"Randy! Randy!" Sean cried. "Get up here, quick!"

Startled, Randy felt his way in the dark over to the stairs and climbed them two at a time. Seconds later, he was in their bedroom. He could barely make out his brother's form silhouetted against the dim glow coming from the slightly open window.

"I'm here," Randy called over to Sean. "What is it?"

"The Ouija board! The pointer is moving!" Sean said excitedly. "Get a flashlight!"

Randy stumbled over to their desk, and found a flashlight. Clicking on the beam, he hurried back to Sean, who was sitting on his bed, his fingers perched on the spirit board's wooden planchet.

"It's spelling something!" Sean cried.

Randy directed the light on the board. The marker was over the letter N. From there it spelled out E-X-T.

"*Next?*" Randy said quizzically.

"Tell me again," Sean said to the board. "Where will the killer strike next?"

As if echoing Sean's question, the marker spelled out N-E-X-T, paused, then spelled out D-O-O-R. Now Randy knew what the board meant. "Next door!" he blurted out. "The killer is going to kill Mr. Lessing!"

With that Randy bolted from the room and raced off through the dark to the phone on his parents' nightstand. But when he picked up the handset, he heard absolutely nothing. No dial tone. Not even static.

"The phones are dead, too!" he reported to Sean racing back into their bedroom. "I'm going to have to go next door and warn Mr. Lessing myself!"

"Ca-can't we call the police?" Sean stammered.

"I told you, the phones are dead!" Randy shouted. "It's up to me to save Mr. Lessing!"

"But what am I supposed to do?" Sean asked anxiously. "I'm scared!"

"Stay here and keep the door locked." Randy said. "Don't let anyone in but me or Mom and Dad." His eyes now accustomed to the darkness, he bounded down the stairs, grabbed a windbreaker and hat from the front closet, then bolted out into the raging storm.

The wind and rain whipped at Randy's face as he ran across the water-soaked yard to Mr. Lessing's side door. At first he tried the doorbell, but seeing that the electricity was out all over the neighborhood, he began pounding on the wooden door.

"Mr. Lessing! Mr. Lessing! Open up!" he cried, his voice nearly lost under the roar of the storm.

Several agonizing seconds later, the lock turned, the door opened, and Mr. Lessing appeared.

"Randy?" he said with surprise. "What are you doing out there in the rain? Quick, come inside before you catch your death."

"No!" Randy cried. "You've got to get out of your house! The serial killer, he's going be here any minute!"

"What are you talking about?" Mr. Lessing said, confused. "How do you know this?"

"Your Ouija board. It knows about the murders," Randy gasped, realizing how ridiculous he sounded even as the words spilled from his mouth. "It told us about the murder in the parking lot before it happened, and then about the one by the river. Just a few minutes ago, it said the killer was going to be next door. That means he's coming *here!*"

Suddenly, a crash that sounded like breaking glass turned Randy's attention back to his own house.

"Unless," Mr. Lessing began nervously, "because I made the board, it means the house next door to *me.*"

A sick, awful feeling knotted up inside Randy's stomach. "Sean!" he cried, already dashing back across the yard to his front door.

"No! Wait!" Mr. Lessing shouted. "I have a cellular phone! Let me call the police!"

But Randy didn't hear him. He was too busy digging his house keys from his pocket, slamming them into the deadbolt lock, turning the knob, and stumbling back into his house. "I'm coming, Sean!" Randy shouted, heading up the stairs. But halfway up, he stopped. Someone was standing on the landing . . . and it *wasn't* his brother.

There in the darkness was a towering form at least six feet tall, dressed in dark clothing. He was holding Sean at knifepoint.

"Where have you been?" the killer said, as if scolding Randy. "I *told* you I was coming."

Responding to Mr. Lessing's call, the police arrived fifteen minutes later, but they found no sign of either brother. However, in the boys' bedroom they discovered a hand-crafted Ouija board on one of the twin beds. Its planchet was poised directly over the word, "Goodbye."

VIRTUAL
MAYHEM

Raymond Gibberman scanned the wall filled with discs and cartridges for every home video game system currently on the market. "So, what's hot?" he asked Tom Cooke, the long-haired clerk who stood behind the glass counter at Galaxy Games.

"Depends on what you're looking for," Tom told his eager twelve-year-old customer. "What do you want? A fighting game? A role-playing game? A shooting game? A flight simulator?"

"I told you, I want whatever's hot," Raymond repeated. "What's the newest game you've got?"

Tom turned around and scanned the expansive display of boxes behind him. "You've got a Super PlayMaster, right?" he asked, referring to the popular new CD-ROM-based game system from Japan.

"Of course," Raymond replied, as if any other choice would have been unthinkable.

"Well, we've got *Chaos Arena II*," Tom said, reaching for a box featuring two wild-looking ninjas engaged in furious combat.

"Bought it last week," Raymond reminded him.

"*Operation: Armageddon?*" Tom asked.

"Got it," Raymond replied.

"*War of the Roaches?*" asked Tom.

"Been there, done that," Raymond said with a sigh.

Tom appeared to ponder the problem for a moment, then his eyes lit up brightly.

"Hey, I just remembered, we got a new shipment in today," he said, moving toward the back of the shop. "I haven't even opened the box yet."

"Great!" Raymond exclaimed. "Maybe it's got some new games."

Raymond watched as Tom disappeared into the back room, then emerged a few moments later carrying a medium-sized cardboard shipping box. Raymond leaned on the counter expectantly as Tom pulled a penknife from his pocket, cut through the packing tape, removed a few handfuls of shredded newspaper, then pulled out a half-dozen shrink-wrapped game boxes.

"Whoa! I've been waiting for this one for weeks!" Tom exclaimed, nearly bursting with excitement. "I'm going to want to play this one *myself!*"

"What is it?" Raymond demanded, prepared to tear one of the games from Tom's hands.

"*Virtual Mayhem,*" said Tom, showing his young customer the game's colorful, action-filled box cover.

"Never heard of it," Raymond replied, somewhat disappointed. An avid reader of video game magazines, he knew all about most of the top new titles months before they ever hit the stores. But although he'd read over a half-dozen fan publications cover-to-cover over the past few weeks, he'd never encountered even one mention of this *Virtual Mayhem.*

"It's been kind of a video industry secret," Tom explained, still unable to take his eyes off the box. "Word has it that, Tohsundo Entertainment, maker of *Virtual Mayhem,* developed this whole new engine that allows the game to play at something like 128 bits."

"You've got to be kidding," Raymond gasped in astonishment. "That's so cool."

Although Raymond was no computer expert, he knew that the term "engine" referred to the software that "drove" a program, and that the higher the bit number, the more realistic it was. The first crude computer games had been designed to run at only 4 bits. That standard had later jumped to 8, 16, 32, and then 64. Each step had brought with it a quantum leap in playing speed and image realism. Raymond had no idea that a 128-bit game was even being developed, especially one that could play on a 64-bit system like the PlayMaster. But if *Virtual Mayhem* operated at that speed, then it had to be the most visually staggering game to ever hit the planet.

"The whole development was top secret," Tom said excitedly. "Tohsundo didn't want anyone stealing their technology or ripping off any of their other ideas. They didn't even want to advertise the game until it was already in the stores."

"So these are the first anywhere?" Raymond asked, his excitement mounting by the second.

"Yeah, I think so," Tom said, equally elated.

"So how much is it?" asked Raymond, already reaching for his wallet.

"The boss hasn't had a chance to price them yet," Tom said, referring to Mr. Gelson, the man who actually owned the video game store. "But based on our usual mark up, plus our usual discount, I'd say I can let you have it for $64.95."

"Sold!" Raymond cried without a moment's hesitation, slapping his money down on the glass countertop. Two minutes later he walked out of Galaxy Games the proud owner of the first *Virtual Mayhem* to be sold anywhere in the United States of America.

● ● ●

"Raymond, it's time for dinner!" his mother called from the kitchen.

"In a minute!" Raymond shouted back from his bedroom. Immediately, the boy returned his attention to the TV screen in front of him. The monitor showed a first-person perspective of a creepy, garbage-strewn alley. When Raymond pushed the buttons on his hand-held controller, the image moved in response to his command. It was as if he himself was moving through the dark, dingy alleyway.

Now, Raymond had played first-person action games before. Such things were nothing new in the world of computer-based entertainment. The difference was the quality of the image. Unlike the blocky, polygon-based perspectives he'd always encountered in past games, this picture was as crisp and clear as anything on a regular TV show. The image even held together when he turned or tilted his perspective up and down. In fact it was like controlling an actual TV camera rather than playing a computer simulation.

In the *Virtual Mayhem* game, the player assumed the role of a detective who was searching for a serial killer who roamed the streets of the city murdering innocent victims in all kinds of bizarre ways. Play involved following the killer around town via a series of clues he left at the scene of each murder, plus fending off the powerful "punks" who also inhabited this particular crime-infested metropolis. In short, *Virtual Mayhem* combined the best elements of role-playing adventure games, fighting games, and brain-twisters. That, coupled with its ultra-realistic sound and graphics, made the game, at least in Raymond's mind, an instant classic.

Continuing to move through the alley, Raymond was shocked to find a fully dressed human skeleton propped up against a fence, its pockets stuffed with fast-food wrappers. He was about to inspect the wrappers for clues when his mother called him again.

"Okay! Okay!" he shouted back. Then he saved his position in the PlayMaster's internal memory, flicked off the power, and headed off for his supper.

In the kitchen, Raymond joined his mother and father, who had already started on their salads.

"Finish your homework?" his dad asked, this usually being the evening's first topic of conversation.

"Finished it at school," Raymond answered. He reached for a roll and then for the tub of margarine. "I got a new PlayMaster game this afternoon. *Virtual Mayhem.* You have *got* to check it out!"

He was about to tell his dad, who enjoyed computer games himself, all about *Virtual Mayhem's* super-realistic graphics and intense storyline when his mother interrupted, "Will you look at that?"

Now everyone turned toward the small color TV that sat on the nearby counter. As usual, the local news was on. The reporter, standing in a grungy alley not unlike the one in Raymond's game, was talking about the police having just discovered a fully clothed human skeleton propped up against a wall, its pockets stuffed with fast-food wrappers.

"How strange," his mother commented. "You think maybe the man died from eating too much fast-food?"

"Maybe, but it usually takes years for a human body to decompose all the way down to a skeleton," his father noted. "Why didn't anyone find the body before?"

Raymond just sat there in stunned silence. What were the chances of him seeing this bizarre scene on TV just minutes after seeing a nearly identical death in *Virtual Mayhem*? Not too great, he figured. There had to be a connection.

"So tell me about this new game," said his father, turning his attention back to his son. "What kind is it?"

Raymond was just about to tell his dad about how the crime being reported on TV was just like the one in *Virtual Mayhem* when he stopped himself short. It was obvious to the boy that whoever the real-life killer was, he had stolen his murderous technique from this new video game. No doubt someone else would soon realize this, too, and that would be followed by the inevitable cry from angry parents and outraged politicians to have the game removed from store shelves before it inspired similar copycat crimes. His folks, concerned for their son's safety, might be taken in by the resulting hysteria and insist that he never play the game again. That was something Raymond couldn't let happen.

So, to keep his parents in the dark about *Virtual Mayhem* for as long as possible, Raymond decided to leave the gory details out of his description.

"Well, it's basically an action-adventure/role-playing game, like *Fate*," he said, referring to a classic computer combat game.

"That's all?" his father asked with a shrug, obviously expecting more.

"That's all," Raymond quickly replied. "So, what happened at the law office today?"

With this question Raymond skillfully changed the subject, and for the rest of the dinner he and his mother listened to his father talk about the various clients he was defending. Later, when Raymond had finished his dessert and his father was just getting into a boring story about insurance fraud, Raymond excused himself and returned to the world of *Virtual Mayhem*. He played the game until he was prompted by his parents—twice—to go to bed. During this time, he discovered two more dead bodies, one which had been killed with a harpoon gun, and the other covered with honey and eaten alive by giant red ants. In each case the crazed killer had left behind a puzzle which led Raymond deeper and deeper into the game.

The next day at school Raymond wasted no time in telling his best friends, Lyle Windsor and Cary Yepsitt, about *Virtual Mayhem*. Not surprisingly, neither of the boys was yet aware of the game, but were thrilled to hear about its amazing capabilities. They listened with rapt attention as Raymond walked them step-by-step through the game's plotline, putting particular emphasis on the bizarre ways the serial killer did away with his victims.

"Hey, I just heard about a guy being eaten alive by red ants," Cary declared immediately after Raymond finished describing this particular murder. "I think it was in the paper this morning."

"And on the radio, I heard about some guy getting killed with a harpoon gun," Lyle added.

"You know what this means, don't you?" Raymond said fearfully. "Some whacko is using *Virtual Mayhem* as a blueprint for his own murder spree."

"You've got to tell the police," Cary insisted. "Maybe they can use the clues in the game to stop the killer before he strikes again!"

Raymond thought this was an excellent idea. He had information that could help catch a killer, and it was his responsibility to bring this information to the proper authorities.

But who was going to believe a twelve-year-old boy? From his experience, he knew adults rarely listened to kids when it came to important matters—like life and death. No, he needed someone to go to the police for him. Someone he could trust.

As soon as school was over, Raymond returned to Galaxy Games. As usual, he found Tom Cooke working behind the counter.

"Raymond, thank goodness you came in!" Tom cried, even before Raymond could open his mouth. "I really need to talk to you. Do you still have *Virtual Mayhem*?"

"Yeah, that's what I came to talk to you about," Raymond began. But again, Tom cut him off.

"You need to bring it back, like right now," Tom insisted. "Otherwise I'm in big trouble."

"Why?" Raymond asked uncomfortably, figuring that this had something to do with the recent murders.

"Tohsundo Entertainment has recalled all their *Virtual Mayhem* games," Tom explained. "It turns out, the ones we got were still prototypes. They got shipped to us by mistake. They don't want anyone to know about the game yet, and they're threatening all kinds of legal trouble if we sell them."

"Someone already knows," Raymond said darkly. "There's been a bunch of murders around town that are just like the ones in *Virtual Mayhem*. I think the killer bought one of these prototypes and decided to play the story out for real." Suddenly, Raymond's eyes lit up. "Tom, how many of these games did Tohsundo accidentally ship out?"

"Just the one box," Tom replied. "The one we got."

"And who else besides me did you sell one to?" Raymond asked insistently. He knew that Tom wrote the name and address of every customer on his sales receipts. This meant that he probably already had the name of the killer in his files.

"Just you," Tom said, much to Raymond's surprise. "I didn't even open one for myself. I was too busy."

Raymond gulped nervously. If he and Tom were the only people outside of Tohsundo who knew about *Virtual Mayhem,* then his theory about a copycat killer was all wrong. Unless the killer *worked* for Tohsundo. But Tohsundo's offices were all in Japan!

"You've got to bring that game back right now, or I'm going to be in *big* trouble," Tom insisted. "We close at nine o'clock. Can you have it back here by then?"

"Yeah, sure," Raymond said absentmindedly, his attention still focused on the mystery that had only gotten deeper these past few minutes. "I'll have it here by nine."

Raymond raced home in record time. Once there, he ran straight to his room, powered up his PlayMaster, and loaded *Virtual Mayhem*. His instincts told him that the secret to the recent murder spree lay somewhere at the heart of this game.

Ignoring both his homework and his mother's insistent orders that he come down for dinner, Raymond focused his full attention on the task before him. Calling upon skills honed through years of intensive video-gaming, he expertly guided his virtual detective through the maze of hazards, death traps, and puzzles that the wily creators of *Virtual Mayhem* had laid out for him.

Oddly, the more he played, the more and more familiar the terrain portrayed in *Virtual Mayhem* seemed to become. With only forty-five minutes to go before he had to return the disc to Galaxy Games, he realized with mounting terror that the neighborhood his virtual character had entered was in fact his *own*!

It was all there—his junior high school, the Buffalo Burger restaurant on Jefferson Street, even Galaxy Games itself!

His mouth suddenly as dry as cotton, Raymond kept his eyes fixed on the glowing TV screen as his first-person perspective led him to the end of a street named Heather Lane—*his* Heather Lane—to a one-story brick-faced house he immediately recognized as his own. Still following the path left him by the killer, he entered the house, moved cautiously through the living room where he saw his own two parents watching television, to the bedroom corridor where he at last saw the object of his search—the serial killer! The sandy-haired man, his eyes glowing an eerie blood red, was standing directly outside Raymond's very own bedroom holding a huge electric drill he no doubt planned to run through his next victim.

"Stop him!" Raymond begged his virtual detective.

But before his computerized alter ego could do anything, the maniac kicked in the door and revved his deadly drill into life.

At that very same instant, Raymond heard his door bang open behind him. Turning, his eyes widened in terror as he saw the serial killer lunging toward him, the whirring drill aimed straight at his heart.

"Ahhhh!" Raymond screamed and leaped aside, managing to avoid death by mere inches. The killer just laughed, turned on Raymond again, and grinned through rotting, crooked teeth as he played with the drill's trigger.

"You're not real," Raymond whispered. "You're just part of the game."

And with that, he pressed the "Power" button on his PlayMaster unit. Instantly, the TV winked off. At the same time, the serial killer also vanished from existence . . . as did Raymond Gibberman.

●　●　●

"Whoa, cool game," twelve-year-old Mike Bermann said to his friend, Niles Johnson.

"That game within a game story was kind of different," Niles agreed. "But I don't know, I thought that ending was kind of weak. I mean, I knew that all Raymond had to do was turn off the video game and the killer would disappear."

"Still, it kind of makes you wonder, how do you know when something is real and something isn't?" Mike mused.

"That's true," Niles agreed. "I mean, we could be just characters in a computer game or in one of those *Scary Stories* books and we'd never know it."

The friends looked at each other for several long, anxious seconds, then broke out in gleeful laughter.

THE ABDUCTION

This story isn't about me, Margo Shane. No, it's about my friend, Debbie O'Malley. It's about how she gave me and everyone else at Jefferson Junior High a scare we'll never forget.

Now, I'd known Debbie ever since the fifth grade. She'd always been a smart girl, and lots of fun to be around. Whether the subject was music, shopping, movies, or boys, Debbie always had something to say, and she often gave her opinions in truly unforgettable ways. This is because Debbie O'Malley was a liar. No, I take that back. A liar is someone who intentionally tells untruths hoping to deceive the listener. It was different with Debbie. When she spun her wild stories, you got the feeling that she actually believed them. Or, at least, she *wanted* to believe them . . . desperately.

For example, one day my friends and I were sitting around the lunch table talking about the new CD just released by the band Poison Oak. We all agreed that, except for two or three stinkers, most of the songs were pretty good. Naturally, Debbie had to put her two cents in . . . and then raise the ante to a dollar.

"You know, I went to school with the lead singer for Poison Oak," she said matter-of-factly.

"Yeah, right," scoffed Pat Eng, who was always the first among us to doubt anything that Debbie ever said. "What's his name?"

"Wilton Boreo," Debbie replied. Well, she was right about that. Poison Oak's lead singer *was* Wilton Boreo, although anyone could know that just by reading the CD's liner notes.

"And where did you two go to school?" I asked, playing along with Debbie's obvious charade.

"Back in Atlantic City, New Jersey," Debbie replied, without even batting an eye. "We were in first grade together. Mrs. Prescott's class."

Again, Debbie was on the mark. From what I knew about Poison Oak, the band *was* from Atlantic City.

"I thought you went to first grade in Beverly Hills," said Darlene Fishburne, trying to catch Debbie in a contradiction. "That's what you told us *last* week."

"That was just my first semester of first grade," Debbie explained confidently. "I finished the year in Atlantic City. You know how it is when your father's a top agent with the FBI. You're moving *all* the time."

I struggled to stifle a laugh. Apparently, Debbie's father was having a hard time making ends meet, because in addition to being a "top agent with the FBI," he was supposedly also an airline pilot, a movie director, a neurosurgeon, a football coach, and an astronaut. He was so busy working, I wondered how the poor man ever found time to have a kid.

"Anyway, I was Wilton's first love," Debbie went on, oblivious to our skepticism. "You know that song on their CD, 'Terri Babe'? He wrote that about *me*."

"Why would he write a song named 'Terri Babe' after *you?*" Pat challenged, her frustration making her red in the face. "Your name is *Debbie!*"

"We had little code names for each other," Debbie calmly replied. "I was Terri, and he was Elton."

"That's it! I give up!" Pat exclaimed, getting to her feet. "What do you think we are, Debbie, *stupid?*"

With that, Pat grabbed what was left of her lunch and stormed off. I turned to Debbie and saw only hurt and confusion on her face. It was like this anytime someone accused her of being a liar. She looked so pained, so innocent—like she was deeply wounded by our distrust of her, even though she'd done everything possible to earn our suspicion.

Maybe it was just that Debbie didn't want to have to face the harsh realities of her own life. You see, the fact was, both of Debbie's parents had been killed by a drunk driver when she was just six years old. Since then, she had lived in a small two-bedroom apartment with her aunt, who worked as an assistant manager over at the local Super Mart. Debbie's life was so ordinary, so colorless, that I really couldn't blame her for wanting to escape into a fantasy world.

Anyway, the Poison Oak incident was soon forgotten, and we all went back to our normal business. For me, that meant struggling my way through geometry and second semester French, and trying desperately to get Paul Crews, who sat three seats away in homeroom, to notice me. Despite my best efforts, I didn't do very well at any of these tasks.

And then, one day, Debbie O'Malley failed to show up for lunch. Concerned, I asked both Pat and Darlene if either one of them had seen her, but neither had. Later, I looked for her in gym class, which was the only class we shared, but again she failed to appear. I quickly concluded she was out sick and would be back in school tomorrow.

But it wasn't until two weeks later that Debbie finally returned. Naturally, we were all relieved to see her alive and well, but on second glance, I realized that she didn't look well at all. In fact, the girl looked awful. Her complexion was pale, her posture stooped, and her eyes had a weird, faraway look to them.

"Debbie, where have you been?" I asked as she joined us at our usual table in the cafeteria. "Were you sick? If you were, you still don't look so good."

"No, Margo, I wasn't sick," Debbie replied, her voice so low it was barely even a whisper.

"So what's the story?" asked Pat, leaning forward with interest. "You get kidnapped by pirates?"

"No, Pat, not pirates," Debbie responded softly.

The other girls and I exchanged nervous glances. Something *had* happened to our friend, something that, by the looks of her, was pretty awful.

"You don't have to talk about it," I said kindly.

"No, that's all right," Debbie said, finally looking up. "I think I *should* talk about it."

"All right," said Darlene, taking a spoonful of raspberry yogurt. "We're listening."

Debbie paused a moment to collect herself. Then she took a deep breath and began to tell her tale.

"It started about two weeks ago on a Tuesday night," she began, referring to the last day we all had gotten together for lunch. "After dinner, Aunt Betty realized we were out of milk, and she asked me to pick up a gallon. As usual, I took my bike."

She paused a moment to take a sip from her juice box. In the seconds that elapsed, I imagined her being run off the road by some crazy hot-rodders or grabbed by some fiend in a black minivan.

"Anyway, I went down Enterprise Way because that's the fastest way to get to the store," Debbie said, referring to a street filled with small industrial buildings, mostly auto repair shops and the like. "This was after seven o'clock, so there was no other traffic on the street. All the businesses were closed down, and the only light around came from the street lamps."

Again I had an awful vision, this time of some wild-eyed maniac leaping out of the shadows waving a tire iron. I shook the awful image from my mind and continued to listen to Debbie's story.

"I was halfway down the street when I noticed a bright white light come on directly above me," Debbie said, her voice suddenly shaky. "At first I thought it was just a street lamp that had snapped on, but—"

"Was it a news or police helicopter?" Pat Eng interrupted. "They're always flying over our house, lighting up the neighborhood and making lots of noise."

"That's what I thought at first, too," Debbie agreed. "Only there weren't any helicopter sounds. In fact, there wasn't any sound at all."

"Were you scared?" Darlene asked, now listening with rapt attention.

"Terrified," Debbie admitted with a nervous laugh. "I knew something was wrong. My gut told me to get out of there as fast as I could."

"So what happened?" I asked, knowing the events in her story were only going to get more amazing.

"I tried to ride away, but I couldn't move," Debbie replied. "It was like all of my muscles were suddenly frozen tight. No matter how hard I tried to get out of there, I was stuck to the spot."

Again, Debbie paused to take a sip of juice while we all waited in anxious silence.

"I must have stood there with my bike for ten, maybe twenty seconds, each second more terrifying than the next," Debbie said, carefully measuring each word. "Then I felt myself being lifted into the air."

"*What?*" Pat cried in disbelief. "That is the most—"

"Let her talk, Pat!" I snapped, caught up in the story as though it was a suspenseful thriller. Then I turned back to Debbie. "It's all right, Deb. Go on."

Debbie smiled at me as if to say "thanks," then continued. "I looked down and could see my bike on the street below. It was getting farther and farther away with each second. Then, all of a sudden, I was inside this small, bright room. The walls looked like they were made out of smooth, frosted glass, and there was this large machine in the center of the room that looked like some kind of weird X-ray machine."

Instinctively, I held my breath. I had seen enough reports about UFOs on TV to know that Debbie was describing a classic "alien abduction." Apparently, Pat

and Darlene were thinking the same thing, for they were now regarding Debbie with expressions of doubt and skepticism. But considering this was Debbie O'Malley talking, that was par for the course.

Still, as familiar as her story was, there was a level of sincerity in her voice I had never heard during any of her other tall tales. Usually, Debbie had a cool, off-handed way of telling her stories that indicated she knew you might not believe her but that she didn't care. This time, however, there was genuine terror in her voice, and it told me that even if the story wasn't true, Debbie herself was absolutely convinced it was.

"I still couldn't move. I couldn't even talk," Debbie went on, her words now coming at a faster pace as she relived the abduction—real or imagined—in her own mind. "Several small beings appeared and led me over to the examination table, where they made me lie down. The creatures were only about three feet tall. They had large, bald heads, black eyes like an insect's, and gray skin that looked like smooth leather."

Again, Debbie was describing a classic "gray," the type of extraterrestrial most commonly associated with UFO abductions. I'd seen the whole thing on a UFO TV special once. Anyway, if I was right, Debbie would now go on to describe a harrowing series of medical experiments, which is exactly what she did. Now, I won't go into details here, but take it from me, they were pretty gruesome. The experiments involved her being poked, prodded, and stuck with long needles. Telling the story seemed to bring back Debbie's memories in such vivid detail that her body shivered and tears welled up in her eyes.

"They were putting something up my nose when I finally blacked out," Debbie stated, wiping away a tear that had slipped down her cheek. "When I woke up, I found myself in the middle of the bean field out near Arbor Road. A policeman found me walking along in a daze and took me home. That was two days ago."

"You mean, you were on that space ship for an entire *week*?" I gasped in disbelief.

"I guess so," Debbie said with a shrug. "It didn't seem that long, but who knows? After I blacked out, I could have been unconscious for days and never even have known about it."

"Why do you think they chose *you*?" Darlene asked, raising a questioning eyebrow.

"I don't know," Debbie confessed. "They took all kinds of samples from all over my body. Maybe they wanted my DNA or something."

"You wouldn't happen to have any proof of any of this, would you?" Pat asked, folding her arms in a "prove it" stance. "I mean, you didn't happen to grab a laser gun or even an alien taco chip while you were up there by any chance?"

Debbie shook her head no.

"Right," Pat said with a sigh. "You know, Debbie, I always knew you were a space cadet, but this proves it. And if either of you believe this stupid story," she added, turning to Darlene and me, "then you're just as cracked as Star Queen here."

The next moment, the bell rang and our lunch period was over. Immediately, Pat and Darlene grabbed their trays and headed for the waste baskets. I hesitated a moment to help Debbie.

"You're going to be okay, aren't you?" I asked.

"Sure," Debbie replied. "You believe me, don't you, Margo? You know I'm not making things up this time."

"Deb, you have to admit it is kind of a crazy story," I said, somewhat embarrassed. "I mean, it sounds like something straight out of *Mysterious Encounters.* Maybe you fell asleep in front of the TV and dreamed the whole thing."

"Fine, don't believe me," Debbie snapped. "But I know it happened. I just wish I could prove it."

"So do I, Debbie," I agreed. "So do I."

●　●　●

Word of Debbie O'Malley's so-called "abduction" spread quickly through the school, and by the time we had gym class, all the girls were talking about it. A few girls believed the story, but most were openly skeptical. No, I take that back. They were more than just skeptical, they were downright *hostile.*

"Hey, O'Malley, when you gonna take us for a ride on your flying saucer?" taunted one of the girls as we warmed up for basketball practice.

"See any little green men lately?" another yelled.

"All right, girls, quiet down and fall in!" shouted our coach, Ms. Lehrman, after blowing her whistle. But even as we moved into our practice lines, all eyes remained on Debbie, who in turn stared down at the ground as if she wanted to be anywhere else but here.

At Ms. Lehrman's direction, we began running drills, dribbling down the court and passing the ball to the next person in line. The exercise went smoothly until it was Debbie's turn. Although she'd never been a star athlete, today she moved even more awkwardly than usual, and when it was her turn to catch the ball, she not only missed it, but it hit her square in the face.

Immediately, we all gathered around Debbie, who'd fallen to the floor. At first, it appeared that she was fine. She was lying, face up, her eyes wide open, her face a complete blank.

I knelt down and took her hand. "Hey, earth to O'Malley," I said, trying to be funny. "You still with us?"

Suddenly, her body gave a convulsive jerk, as if it had just been jolted with electricity. Startled, I released her hand and jumped back to my feet.

"Everyone, get back!" Ms. Lehrman ordered as Debbie's entire body went into uncontrolled spasms. "Someone call 911! Tell them we have a fourteen-year-old girl who's having a seizure!"

The girl closest to the door raced for the exit. At the same time, I looked back at Debbie and was horrified to see her body steaming like butter burning in a hot frying pan. Then her features began to melt away as her body sunk in on itself like a deflating balloon.

Several girls screamed, but I was too frightened to even do that. Instead, I just watched in silent terror as my friend—or the thing I *thought* was my friend—dissolved away into a pile of thick, green goo.

●   ●   ●

It was well after six o'clock when I was finally able to go home. The police had interviewed me and the other members of our gym class for several hours, then some government people came in and did the same thing. I told them Debbie's story about being abducted by aliens, and how none of us had believed her. I ended by guessing that the "Debbie" we'd talked to had been some kind of clone the aliens had created using her DNA samples. One of the government people called that theory "imaginative."

Walking home an hour after sunset, I couldn't help but wonder where the *real* Debbie O'Malley might be right now. Was she still aboard that strange alien spaceship? Had she been taken to another planet? Or, worst of all, was that pile of steaming slime all that was left of the *real* Debbie?

I was considering all these terrifying possibilities when, looking down, I noticed my shadow standing out brightly against the sidewalk below. Startled, I looked up—and saw a hot white light shining down directly above me. And there was no sound.

THE SUBSTITUTION

Mrs. Grunchmacher cleared her throat. "I don't mean to disturb you, Trevor," she said sarcastically, "but could you tell the class about the Turner Thesis?"

Thirteen-year-old Trevor Krabbe looked up from the doodles he'd been making in his notebook. From a series of disconnected squares and triangles, he had artistically fashioned a huge, dinosaurlike monster straight out of an old Japanese horror movie. If a psychiatrist were to see this and the other horrific drawings in Trevor's notebook, he might conclude that the boy had a very sick and twisted imagination. But to Trevor the drawings merely represented the normal frustrations of a healthy, all-American male who was bored silly with American history. At least, he was bored with the way Mrs. Grunchmacher taught it.

"The Turner Thesis, Trevor?" his stern, gray-haired teacher repeated impatiently.

"Um, could you rephrase the question?" Trevor asked innocently.

"Do you know what the Turner Thesis is?" Mrs. Grunchmacher said through clenched teeth. "Manifest Destiny? Westward expansion? Does any of this sound familiar, or have I been wasting my time?"

Trevor sunk into his chair and averted his eyes. The truth was, he had no idea what Mrs. Grunchmacher was talking about, but felt it was better to stay silent rather than admit he'd been daydreaming for the entire period.

Mrs. Grunchmacher heaved a frustrated sigh, then turned to address the other students, who looked just as lost as Trevor. "You know, education is a two-way street. I can stand up here and talk all I want, but it's not going to do a bit of good unless you choose to pay attention. You have to *want* to learn. You have to make an *effort*. I can't do it all myself."

"Oh, yeah?" Trevor cried, suddenly leaping to his feet. "Well, maybe we would pay attention if you said something *interesting*! If you didn't babble on and on about things that didn't make any difference today!"

Actually, Trevor didn't really say this. He *wanted* to say it. He was *desperate* to say it. But his combination of fear, shyness, and perhaps common sense prevented him from doing so. Instead, he just sunk lower and lower into his chair and silently wished that Mrs. Grunchmacher would simply vanish off the face of the earth. Maybe then school might not be the living nightmare he currently found it to be.

"All right, Trevor," Mrs. Grunchmacher said, returning her attention to him alone. "Just to show me that my efforts have not been totally wasted, I want a five-page report from you on the Turner Thesis on my desk tomorrow morning."

"But I can't—" Trevor began.

"There's no such word as *can't* in my classroom," Mrs. Grunchmacher snapped, cutting him off. "You have to demand one hundred percent from yourself. Remember, success only comes from high expectations."

"Yes, ma'am," Trevor grumbled, secretly wishing for the day when the old bat would finally be out of his life forever.

●　●　●

"Mrs. Grunchmacher has got to be at least sixty years old," Trevor's friend Norbert LaGrange noted as the two of them rode the bus home from school that afternoon. "Statistically speaking, she could drop dead at any time."

Norbert was also in Mrs. Grunchmacher's class and shared Trevor's extreme dislike of the old woman.

"I don't want her to die," Trevor insisted. "I just want her to go away. You know, like retire. Move to Bora Bora or something."

"It's not gonna happen," Norbert stated. "We're not that lucky."

Trevor figured that if Mrs. Grunchmacher wasn't going to disappear, then at least *he* could come down with the flu and not have to go to school for the rest of the week. Yes, even headaches, muscle aches, chills, and nausea were starting to look better than a single day with that awful old school teacher.

Unfortunately, the next morning Trevor Krabbe was in perfect health. He had no choice but to get dressed, have breakfast, pack up his books, and catch the bus to school. Sitting with Norbert, Trevor was halfway to Wendell Wilkie Junior High when he realized, much to his horror, that he'd completely forgotten about the paper Mrs. Grunchmacher had assigned him to write.

"Mrs. Grunchmacher is going to eat you alive!" Norbert exclaimed after Trevor told him about the mistake. "Boy, I'd hate to be in your shoes."

"Maybe she forgot about it," Trevor said hopefully.

"Not likely," Norbert said with a ghoulish laugh. "She's still after my big brother Jack about a social studies paper he forgot to turn in—and that was five years ago!"

Trevor's legs were trembling with fear when he entered his homeroom class and took his usual seat. As class time approached, he sunk even lower than normal in his chair, hoping that when she arrived, Mrs. Grunchmacher wouldn't notice him.

And then, at 8:30 A.M. on the nose, something unexpected happened. Mrs. Grunchmacher failed to appear. Five minutes later, the teacher was still nowhere to be seen.

She's not coming! thought Trevor, joy rising in his heart. *Maybe she had car trouble, or she's sick, or maybe—she actually disappeared!*

Trevor was still imagining all the possible reasons for Mrs. Grunchmacher's absence when a young, beautiful woman with long black hair strode into the classroom and stopped in front of the teacher's desk.

"May I have your attention, please," she said with a dazzling smile, her voice as beautiful as she was. "My name is Ms. Wintergreen. I'll be your substitute today."

For the first time in weeks, Trevor actually bolted up straight in his chair, both stunned by the wonderful news and taken by the substitute's stunning good looks. Then he slowly raised his hand. "Uh, excuse me," he said. "But is Mrs. Grunchmacher sick?"

"To tell you the truth, I really don't know," Ms. Wintergreen admitted. "Your principal, Mrs. Wilhite, called me about an hour ago and asked me to come in. Now, let's get to our work, shall we?"

Over the next forty minutes, a miracle happened. For the first time since he entered the seventh grade, Trevor Krabbe paid attention during a history lecture. Even more amazing, he actually *enjoyed* it. Unlike Mrs. Grunchmacher, who always spoke in the same dull, uninspired monotone, and who always got bogged down in endless, unimportant details, Ms. Wintergreen taught the class with the energy and enthusiasm of a stage actress. Talking about historical ideas, attitudes, and emotions in such a way that it made Trevor actually *feel* something for the period she was talking about, the substitute made him actually *eager* to learn more. And after school, he found out Norbert felt the same way.

"Isn't Ms. Wintergreen the greatest?" Norbert exclaimed as the two rode home on the bus later that day after school. "I mean, I actually *care* about the American pioneers!"

"On a scale of one to ten, I'd say she's a solid twenty-five!" Trevor replied. Then his expression darkened. "I hope this isn't her only day. I mean, if Mrs. Grunchmacher comes back tomorrow, I don't think I'll be able to stand it."

"I know," Norbert agreed. "Just one day, and we've been spoiled!"

"For life," Trevor added. Turning to the window, he silently wished that Mrs. Grunchmacher would *never* come back, that Ms. Wintergreen would be his homeroom teacher for the rest of the semester. Of course, he realized that was too much to expect. But then, as Mrs. Grunchmacher was fond of saying, success only comes from high expectations.

● ● ●

The next morning Trevor crept cautiously into his classroom like a young medieval knight entering the lair of a deadly dragon. Although he fervently hoped that Ms. Wintergreen would return, he knew it was far more likely that Mrs. Grunchmacher would be back, her recent illness having made her meaner and more ornery than ever.

But to his delight, he found Ms. Wintergreen seated at the desk preparing her notes for the day.

"Hi, Ms. Wintergreen!" Trevor said with a smile. "I'm really glad you're back."

"I'm happy to be here," she replied warmly. "Everyone here has been so nice to me. And the class is so attentive. It makes it a pleasure to teach."

"Well, you make it a pleasure to learn," Trevor said, blushing when he realized that he sounded like a teacher's pet. Embarrassed, he hurried to his desk.

When the bell rang three minutes later and all the students had taken their seats, Ms. Wintergreen closed the door and began her instruction.

"First of all, I'd like to announce that Wendy Radcliffe and Joseph Morgenstern are no longer in this class," she said pleasantly.

Trevor perked up in surprise. Although he didn't know either Wendy or Joseph very well—both of the kids had been goof-offs who'd kept pretty much to themselves—he hadn't heard any talk about either of them moving or transferring to another school.

"In their place, I'd like to welcome two new students to our class," the substitute teacher went on in her lilting voice. "Let's say hello to Vicky Carswell and Bradley McShane."

Trevor and the other kids turned to see two new kids sitting at Wendy's and Joseph's old desks. Both kids were unusually good-looking and perfectly dressed. Together, they nodded to the class and flashed identical, picture-perfect smiles.

"Now, let's get back to American history, shall we?" said Ms. Wintergreen, opening her textbook. "Today I'd like to discuss the conflicts between the European settlers and the Native Americans."

Again, Ms. Wintergreen launched into a wonderful history lecture. But this time, Trevor's attention started to wander. He couldn't help but glance back at the new kids, wondering where they might have come from, and where Wendy and Joseph had gone.

"Don't you think its weird that these two new kids showed up on the same day Wendy and Joseph left?" Trevor asked Norbert during their bus ride home.

"A little," Norbert agreed. "But weird things happen. Like those twins who were separated at birth, grew up in totally different parts of the country, and ended up living right next door to each other!"

"What's your point?" Trevor demanded impatiently.

"I'm just saying don't sweat it," Norbert advised. "This is a weird world. But that's no reason to get all paranoid."

Trevor decided to take his friend's advice—until the next morning when he found that five more students in his class had been "substituted" by new kids. All of them were good-looking, perfectly groomed, sweet-natured, and unfailingly cheery . . . just like the amazing Ms. Wintergreen.

This time even Norbert had to admit that something seriously weird was going on. Sitting at their cafeteria table during lunch, the two boys discussed what their next move should be.

"We have to talk to the principal," Norbert insisted. "She's bound to know what's going on."

"But what if the principal is in on it?" Trevor asked. "*She's* the one who called Ms. Wintergreen in the first place. Maybe Mrs. Wilhite is just using Ms. Wintergreen to—"

"To *what?*" Norbert demanded, getting upset. "All we know is that new kids are replacing old ones."

"Just like Mrs. Grunchmacher was replaced," Trevor said. And then it hit him. "Norbert, think about this. So far, who has disappeared? First it was Mrs. Grunchmacher, someone no one could stand. Then it was Wendy Radcliffe and Joseph Morgenstern, two of the worst students in the class."

"Even worse than we are," Norbert noted.

"That's right, even worse than we are," Trevor agreed, his agitation rising. "Then five more kids went, and none of them were exactly straight-A students."

"So what are you saying, Trev?" Norbert asked, his eyes filled with fear. "That they're getting rid of all the bad students and substituting them with good ones? That maybe we'll be next?"

"Could be," said Trevor, now glancing around as if half-expecting someone to be creeping up behind him with a sledgehammer and a butterfly net. "Maybe this is their way of raising the school's test averages. By getting rid of all the losers, maybe they can get more money from the school board or something."

"Okay, but what happens to all the bad students?" asked Norbert. "What do they do, send them to another school? Throw them into a big pit? What?"

"Unless we get our grades up really fast, something tells me we'll soon find out," Trevor replied grimly.

● ● ●

The next morning Trevor headed off to school feeling like a condemned man about to face a firing squad. From the moment he stepped out his front door he kept his eyes fixed forward, his face frozen in an expression of dark determination as he struggled to mentally prepare himself for whatever awful fate lay ahead.

Aboard the school bus, he rode alone. Norbert LaGrange had not gotten on at his usual stop, indicating to Trevor that whatever forces were making the students of Mrs. Grunchmacher's class disappear had already gotten to his friend. His feelings of dread rose again when he walked stiffly into his class and saw a tall, well-dressed boy sitting in Norbert's usual chair. In fact, the classroom was now filled with cute, squeaky-clean kids, all of whom had the same perfect posture, the same attentive expressions, and the same achingly sweet, pearly-white smiles. There wasn't a familiar face among them.

"Come on in, Trevor," Ms. Wintergreen called from her desk. "We're all just dying to get started today."

With this, Trevor snapped. Spinning on his heels, he bolted like a madman down the hall, vaulted down the stairs, and burst into the administration office.

"I've got to talk to Principal Wilhite!" he gasped to the three startled-looking secretaries. "It's a matter of life or death!"

"I'm sorry," one of the secretaries replied. "But Mrs. Wilhite isn't with us anymore."

The next moment the door to the principal's office opened and a stunningly beautiful woman wearing a perfectly tailored designer suit and a movie-star smile stepped into view.

"Why, hello, Trevor," she said in a rich, musical voice. "I'm the new principal, Ms. Cornflower. And I've been waiting for you." She reached her perfectly manicured fingers toward him.

"Noooooooo!" Trevor screamed. "I am not going to be substituted."

Turning around, he bolted back out into the hall, sprinted to the school's main entrance, threw open the front door, ran down the front steps . . . and suddenly found himself tumbling through a black void.

Kicking his arms and legs wildly as a cold wind whipped past his face, Trevor turned and looked up in terror to see his school getting smaller and smaller, like a picture disappearing into a bottomless well. Only it was Trevor who was falling, and who would likely continue to fall until the end of time. For as the last bit of light vanished above him and he found himself enveloped in frigid blackness, Trevor realized that through a combination of forces he would likely never understand, he had in fact just disappeared off the edge of the earth.

● ● ●

"So who can tell me about the Turner Thesis?" Ms. Wintergreen asked her class of attentive seventh graders. Every hand in the room went up. She pointed to the student seated in the second row of the third aisle. "Mark?"

Mark Miller, the handsome, well-dressed boy who sat at the desk once occupied by the now-forgotten Trevor Krabbe, smiled brightly as he began to discuss nineteenth century historian Frederick Turner and his ideas about the American frontier. The other students, all of whom were just as attractive and sharply attired as Mark, listened with rapt attention. They were all perfect students with a perfect teacher in what had finally become a perfect class.

Meanwhile, somewhere far, far away, Trevor Krabbe sank lower and lower into his seat. There, at the front of a classroom identical to the one he'd been miserable in at Wendell Wilkie Junior High, was old Mrs. Grunchmacher babbling on and on about things he'd never care about or understand, even if he lived for a million years. And in this new world—identical to the one Trevor had just disappeared from, except for the perfect people that had replaced him and his doomed classmates—living for a million years was eminently possible.